ETERNITY'S CHOICE

SIENNA BLAKE

CONTENTS

1

CHAPTER 1

I know how I die. I know when, too.

It's going to happen less than two months from now, a few weeks after my eighteenth birthday and right before my family thinks I'm supposed to start college. My aunt will be devastated. Not because of the death thing, but because she hates wearing black. Plus, me dying means she won't get to host The Event of the Year to impress all of her friends before sending me off to Harvard. She's been counting on outdoing Mrs. Jensen, my ex-best-friend Selena's mother, since my sophomore year. That's when the Jensens had their big moving-to-L.A. party that robbed my aunt of her Best-Hostess-on-the-Cul-de-Sac title, or so she thinks. I'm pretty sure no one else cares. It was the same night Selena had it out with me.

My uncle might be sad for a while, but he'll get over it. He's a surgeon. I've never seen him cry.

I'm not sick or anything, and I'm not planning my end. I just know what's going to happen. Just like I knew my parents wouldn't be coming home that afternoon when I was six and that the days of Disneyland and ice cream floats would end the second my aunt got ahold of me. And just like I know right now if the concert I'm at is the last one I'll go to, I'm going to be mega-pissed. I can't see anything. Typical.

I'm certain there's some universal law that if you're under five-foot-four and standing close to the stage at an outdoor concert, some insanely tall person will come stand right in front of you. It rarely fails. Tonight's answer to the law is blond and around six feet tall, give or take an inch. He looks to be about my age, which means he should have the decency to at least pretend to be a gentleman and not stand in front of a girl. L.A. boys are the worst, I swear, even though I once thought no boys could be worse than the brats I went to school with in Boston. I changed my mind last week when some clown at the LAX baggage claim stepped on my foot before pushing me out of the way. And I mean that literally, since he was actually dressed as a clown. Welcome to L.A. and the start of my summer vacation.

The guy in front of me now is cute and all—hot, actually, in that way where I can just tell most girls would let him get away with almost anything—but I'm not most girls and he's still in my way. I'd much rather be watching the stage than studying his ironic T-shirt and the back of his head, both of which are annoying me to no end. Buddy, move over.

He's glued to his phone, though, completely oblivious and texting away. I think for a second, blowing a strand of my chestnut-brown hair out of my face. Then I try stepping to the side. My foot lands right on the foot of the girl standing next to me.

"Sorry," I mumble, retreating. The girl's lips smile, but her eyes don't. She has one on me, though, because I'm not smiling. I'm back to staring at this guy's head. He's still texting.

I lift my heels off of the ground so I can stand on tiptoe. Just when I can see the band's singer, an arm shoots up, phone in hand, obstructing my view once more. Great. Him again. It figures he's part of the camera phone fanarazzi. He's probably live-tweeting the entire show, too.

I have two options here that I can see, other than giving up and moving farther away from the stage to watch the show. I can stay here and fight the urge to kick this guy, or I can try to squeeze in front of him. Maybe I can accidentally connect my foot with his leg on my way by. Option two it is. I square my shoulders and turn my body sideways, then try to wedge myself between him and the girl standing next to him.

He barely glances at me when I bump into him, but the girl fixes me with what I'm sure is her version of a death stare. I force the corners of my lips to turn up into a smile, or at least what I hope passes for one.

"Sorry," I say. I'm not, but she doesn't need to know that. "I'm not trying to get in front of you, I just couldn't see over the guy beside you."

A knowing look appears on her face. She gets it—she's even short-er than I am. "No problem," she replies, taking a step to the side to give me more room.

"Thanks. I'm Cassidy, by the way." I don't really want to make friends with her, but I've learned that the more polite I am to the people I shove, the less likely I am to get shoved back or punched. She nods and turns her head back to the stage.

I'm elbow-to-elbow with the guy now, and I'm not budging. He takes a step backward after a few minutes pass. It's about time. I want to tell him that but I keep my mouth shut, quickly scooting over to claim the empty spot so I can give the girl beside me some breathing room. Victory.

Now that I can see the stage, the show is freaking amazing. Lazy Monday is my favorite band. I've never seen them play before tonight but I have every album they've released and a few bootlegs, and I know the words to all of their songs. I was fifteen the first time I heard one of their songs on the radio in my aunt's car. It was the only bright spot in my day after being held hostage for back-to-school shopping at a bunch of snooty little boutiques. Turning up the volume on the Lazy Monday song won me the iciest of icy looks and a station-change to something classical. The obvious thing to do was to download the song when I got home and blast it from my bedroom for the next four months. I doubt my aunt misses my music collection very much now that it's here with me in L.A., thousands of miles away from her house in Boston. I doubt she misses me much, either.

The universal law of concerts kicks in again during the show's encore, but that's usually how it goes. People farther back in the crowd surge forward for their chance to see some band sweat, and some of them try to push past me. There's no point in fighting this many people so I take a step backward, stumbling when my foot slides on something on the ground. I look down and see somebody's University of Southern California student card beside my shoe.

I bend over to pick it up, bumping arms with the wall of people around me on the way down and again when I stand back up. The photo on the card tells me it belongs to the guy who was blocking my view at the start of the show. It probably fell out of his pocket one of the seventy-spillion or so times he pulled out his phone. It serves him right to lose it, but I turn around anyway to see if he's still close by. None of the faces behind me look familiar. I rise up on the balls of my feet to see if he's been nudged a few rows back but still don't see him. Oh well, I tried.

I think about dropping the card back on the ground. Something makes me stop and glance at the name printed beside the photo, though. Wait. I bring the card closer to my face, reading it again just to be sure.

Riley Davis. It can't be. But it figures that it is.

I study the photo, closer this time, looking for any hint that it's not someone else who just happens to live in the same city and have the same name. It's him, or at least I think it is. I turn around to search the crowd again, but there's still no sign of Riley Davis. It's not lost on me that just a few minutes ago, I would have been more than happy to never see the back of his head again. Now my stomach is sinking because I don't spot him anywhere.

He can't disappear. I've waited almost eighteen years to find him, even though I didn't know his name until last week. I was starting to think he didn't exist since I couldn't find him on the internet. I mean, who can't you find on the internet? People who don't exist, that's who.

He exists, though, and he's gone. I'd curse, but I'm trying to be better about that since I'm dying soon. Not that swearing would keep me from what comes next, the place most people here call the afterlife. They're wrong about that, by the way. It's actually called The Life-After, and the only thing keeping me from getting there is one Mr. Riley Davis. I really don't have time for him to just up and vanish. He doesn't have time for it either, but he doesn't know that. If I don't find him and help him, he'll die. I mean, he'll die at some point anyway since everybody does. It won't be the right time for him, though, and then he'll end up just like me and be forced to come back here for a second time. I won't end up anywhere—not here or The Life-After. I'll just be gone forever.

Tucking the card in my purse, I push past the sea of people around me who are still trying to get closer to the stage. Riley couldn't have gotten very far, and I have to find him.

I pull into the driveway in front of my house just before eleven o'clock. Riley's student card is still in my purse and he's still missing, damn him. So much for not cursing. There has to be a way to find him again, even in this city of millions.

"Sleep on it," I tell myself, pulling the keys from the ignition and getting out of the car.

My footsteps echo in the driveway as I walk up to the front stoop of the house that officially becomes mine on my eighteenth birthday. Not that it will be mine for all that long. I lived in this house once before, until my parents died and I was whisked away to Boston.

Once I'm inside, I kick my shoes into a corner and then head for the kitchen, taking a deep breath as I walk down the hall. I hold it for a moment, trying to clear my mind so I can relax. My breath turns into a yelp on its way out of my lungs.

I'm not alone in my house.

2

CHAPTER 2

"Way to announce yourself," I hiss at Noah.

He only smiles, raising his head up from the newspaper that's scattered across the kitchen table. He's wearing the same clothes he always does, the brown pinstripe suit and fedora that make him look like he walked straight out of the 1930s and into my house.

Noah is my advisor, assigned to watch over me while I'm here in this life. He was the one to greet me after I died and found myself in The Life-After. My name was Anna Merrick then, and I was a TV star, one of those young Hollywood actresses the tabloids called an "up-and-comer" and "one to watch." People recognized me on the street and everything. Dying at eighteen wasn't part of my big career plan. Stuff happens sometimes.

"You didn't see the feather I left by the front door?" Noah asks. He takes off his fedora and sets it on the table.

He means an indigo feather, I know. He always leaves one for me to find when he's about to show up out of nowhere. I must have missed it this time. He calls the feathers a courtesy notice that he's around, and I call them warnings of visits from my warden. He doesn't think that's funny.

"You're a little late for the housewarming. I've already been here for a week." I lean against the kitchen island, watching him. "You brought gifts, right?"

"I think you found your gift tonight."

"Riley?" I ask. His mouth quirks up into a smile, and I guess that's my answer. "Thanks for assigning me some guy I wanted to kick at first sight."

"It will be good for you," he replies. Right.

"Broccoli is good for me, but that doesn't mean I have to like it." He gives me a warning look. "What? I'm a second-timer, not an angel."

He frowns but doesn't say anything, and that's probably because he knows I'm right. If I were an angel, I'd be in The Life-After and free to come and go. I sure wouldn't be stuck here for a second time. I turn my back to him and walk over to the fridge, catching sight of my reflection in a mirrored magnet that's stuck to the door. There's no mistaking the irritation in my sea-blue eyes.

"Want grilled cheese?" I call over my shoulder.

"Only if you're not cooking." He chuckles at his own joke.

"Funny." I open the fridge door and grab cheese slices and a stick of butter from one of the shelves. "Anything you're here for, other than slinging insults?"

"I just popped in to see how you are. It's part of the job, you know."

"It must have slipped my mind." I walk over to the stove.

He watches me spread butter onto a slice of bread. I know he can hear what's on my mind, but he's waiting for me to say it. The guy just never makes it easy.

"Why didn't I know that was Riley tonight?" I ask.

"You know it now." A typical Noah answer. Why I bother asking him questions is beyond me.

"It's a little late now, don't you think? He was already gone by the time I figured it out, or did you miss that part?"

"You'll find him again." He sounds so calm. It must be nice.

"You realize I have less than two months to do that?" You'd think he would get that we're cutting it way too close for me to feel good about this, but he just shrugs. Awesome.

"You'll find him," he repeats. "Just watch for the signs."

"What's that supposed to mean?" I reach for a frying pan that's hanging on a rack beside the stove. When Noah doesn't answer, I put the pan down and turn around to look at him. He's not sitting at the table anymore, and he isn't anywhere else in the kitchen. I already know he's on his way back to The Life-After.

"Figures," I mumble. This is the guy who wouldn't even tell me Riley's name until last week. That's about as helpful as he's going to be. I don't feel so hungry anymore.

I walk over to the table. Noah's newspaper is still there, open to the last page he was reading. The entertainment headlines stare up at me.

"That's some thought-provoking reading," I mumble, but I pluck the newspaper up from the table anyway and head out of the kitchen. I might need something mindless to help me sleep tonight.

After a trip to the bathroom to brush my teeth, I climb into bed. I don't get under the covers, though, but sit cross-legged on top of them, my back propped up against a few pillows. I let my eyes close. It's not long before I see threads of golden light, the glow growing brighter until it's nearly blinding. Then I'm floating in a sea of sparkling colors, most never seen by anyone who hasn't been to

The Life-After. The golden light and new colors were the first things I saw after I died. Noah was the second.

Tonight while I connect, I'm drawn into a memory of arriving in The Life-After as Anna, another lifetime ago.

I know there was a car crash. I don't see a car anywhere, though, and I'm not bleeding or in any kind of pain. I was, though. I know that. There was glass and blood everywhere. My blood. It hurt a lot, and then I blacked out.

I don't even know where I am, except this definitely isn't my wrecked car on the highway, and it sure isn't a hospital. It kind of looks like I'm gazing out over L.A. from somewhere up in the Hollywood Hills. There aren't any buildings below me, though, or even a coastline in the distance. All I can see for miles are what look like thousands or maybe even millions of lights, and most are colors I've never seen before. I had no idea colors could even look like this.

I could be in a coma, I guess, or hopped up on some really good pain drugs. This could be a hallucination or a dream.

"You're not hallucinating, Anna. All of this is real."

The voice comes from out of nowhere. It should probably startle me since I almost always scare easily, but it doesn't. All I feel is calm. When I turn my head to find the owner of the voice, I see one of the tiny lights expand and change form until there's a man standing in front of me. He's wearing a brown suit and fedora, a handkerchief neatly folded and peeking out of his front pocket.

I'm definitely not in Hollywood anymore. Or if I am, this is one crazy soundstage with the most well-designed set I've ever seen.

The man chuckles. "It's not Hollywood, either."

Weird. I didn't think I'd said that out loud.

"You didn't," he answers. "I can hear your thoughts."

A magically morphing thought-reader in the middle of some kind of psychedelic light show. Yeah, I'm not ruling out the pain drugs just yet.

"Where am I?" I start to get to my feet, but the man shakes his head, putting a hand up to stop me. He comes to sit beside me, and it's then I realize we're sitting on what looks like hundreds and hundreds of crystals fused together. Whatever this is, it's not hard or even bumpy. It's more like sitting on a big comfy sofa. I'm not sure my mind could make this up, drugs or not.

"You probably call this the afterlife," the man tells me. "We call it The Life-After."

"Oh." There's the calm again. Any time I've watched a movie or read a book where someone found out they died, I've been sure that if I ever found myself in the same situation, I'd react the way those characters did. Shock and denial. Disbelief. A zillion questions. But this is nothing like that at all.

"I'm Noah," he says.

"Anna," I reply, but then remember he knows that. He's already called me by name.

I look around me and then back at Noah. "Do you live here?" I ask. It's probably a dumb question. No one where I came from could transform from a dot of light into a person.

"We all live here eventually. It's different from what you expected, I'm sure."

He takes off his fedora, revealing a shock of dark brown hair. He doesn't look like he could be more than forty years old. If he lives here, though, he must be older than that.

"You can choose how you appear to others," he says, apparently reading my thoughts again. "Appearance doesn't matter here. Energy is what we are, and it's your energy that's recognized. This is just a shell."

"Got it," I say. That's a lie, because I'm not sure I get it at all. I don't know what I expected, to tell the truth. Dying isn't something I've thought about much, other than when I watched those movies and read those books. "It's pretty here," I add.

"More than you know. You can't see most of it."

I twist my body to look behind me. There are lights on that side, too. They're in every direction I look, so I don't know what it is this guy thinks I'm missing.

"I can see tons of lights," I inform him.

"There's a lot more to it than the lights."

I turn my head to the left and then to the right. Maybe he means the crystal-looking things.

"More than what we're sitting on, too." Okay, seriously. I have to figure out how he does the thought-reading thing. This seems a little one-sided, if you ask me.

"There are other things here?" I'm still not sure I believe him. If there's something else around me, I'd have to be able to see it or I'd walk right into it. Wouldn't I?

He smiles. "Strange, I know. That's how it always is, though. If you'd been ready, you could have seen a lot of what you're seeing right now during your time in The Before."

"The Before?" I ask.

"The place you came from that you thought was your life. We call it that because it's really just the time that comes before all of this." He motions to everything in front of us. "Well, this and everything you can't see yet."

I wave my hand through the air in front of me, waiting to hit some object that's supposedly visible to him but not me. There's only empty space, and now I'm curious.

"When will I be ready to see the rest of it? In a few days?"

He studies me. I can't say I'm crazy about the look on his face. I can tell he's trying to decide if I'll like what I'm about to hear.

"You're not really supposed to be here," he finally says.

3

CHAPTER 3

"No kidding," I answer. "I was in the middle of shooting a movie, you know. I wasn't supposed to crash my car."

"The car crash was supposed to happen. We caused it."

I stare at him. "You just said I'm not supposed to be here. Why would you make me die?" There had better be a good reason for this, because the movie I'm filming is supposed to skyrocket me to Hollywood's A-list. I know I would be ticked off beyond belief if I could just feel something other than complete calm.

Noah folds his hands together, resting them on his lap. He looks me straight in the eyes. "There was a cosmic accident."

An accident. I should be seething. "The car crash, you mean?"

"The car crash wasn't the cosmic accident," he replies. Okay then. I wait for him to say something else, but he doesn't.

"What was it?" I prompt.

He's not looking me in the eyes anymore. This isn't a good sign.

"Meeting David Burns."

I wait for what usually happens when someone mentions David—the feeling like I can't breathe and someone is stabbing right through me with a thousand little knives. It doesn't come.

"You won't feel pain here," Noah says. I guess that explains it.

"That would have helped a couple of months ago," I mutter.

The day David vanished just about destroyed me. I think about where I am right now and what I'm hearing. Correction. If I died, then David's disappearance actually did destroy me.

"The Before is different," he continues. "The energy is different. While you're here, you won't feel the things you felt there."

While I'm here? I expect him to respond to that thought, too, but he doesn't.

"So what about David?" I ask.

"You weren't supposed to meet him."

I wait for a second, but I don't feel any of the things I brace myself for. It seems Noah is right. Pain doesn't happen here. If anything were going to hurt me, it would be hearing I was never supposed to meet the person I loved more than breathing.

I want to ask why I wasn't supposed to meet him, but Noah doesn't give me a chance.

"David was what we call a second-timer," he explains. "He'd already had one turn in The Before as somebody else, and then he went back. He didn't return to The Life-After when he was supposed to. If he had, your paths would never have crossed and you wouldn't be here now."

I pretend not to hear the last part, since I know he has to be wrong. You can't tell someone they were never supposed to meet the love of their life.

"He was reincarnated?" I ask instead.

"If that's how you understand it."

"Is he here now?" I can't help but feel a twinge of excitement. David vanished without a trace, which means he has to be here, and now I can see him again. That's something I never believed possible.

"No."

My excitement fades. "So he's still there, then? In The Before?" This makes less sense, but none of what's happening right now is what I would call crystal clear.

"It's a little more complicated than that." I wait for Noah to say more, but he doesn't.

"Is he an angel?" As much as I love him, this is a little hard to imagine. David loves motorcycles and leather jackets, and singing in bands. There's nothing to say an angel can't like those things, I guess. That's just not what I grew up picturing when I thought of angels.

"He's definitely not an angel," Noah replies.

"Are you an angel?"

He shakes his head. "I'm an advisor."

That's a new one. Angels and reincarnation I've at least heard of.

"I don't know what that is," I admit.

"There are different levels of energy you can achieve here in The Life-After," he tells me. "Angels are the most evolved. The highest form of energy, you might say. They can see things even I can't see. Next are advisors like me, and then second-timers."

Advisors, angels, and second-timers. And this whole world of lights and things I can't see. It's a lot to take in.

"What does an advisor do?" I ask.

"Advisors are assigned to second-timers. They watch over them and help them when they go back to The Before."

He keeps his eyes on me. I hear his words echo in my mind. They watch over them and help them when they go back to The Before. Go back. He can't mean me.

"Second-timers are people who choose to go back, right?" I ask.

The look I don't like appears on his face again. I know I'm in trouble when he presses his lips together and shifts his eyes away from me, staring out over the lights.

"There are two types of people who become second-timers," he says. "The first type are those who come here when they're ready for The Life-After, but then volunteer to return to The Before and help the people there who need a hand."

"And the second type?" I have a feeling I don't want to hear his answer.

"They're a little more rare. The second type are the people whose lives have gotten so far off track that we have to intervene. It's usually because something happened to them that we didn't see coming, so we didn't have a second-timer assigned to help them get through it. We call that a cosmic accident."

"Like with me," I say.

"Like with you," he replies. Great.

"So I go back to my life?" I ask. "I heal from my accident, go back to acting, and help someone?"

He hesitates. "Not exactly."

"What exactly, then?"

The silence lasts a moment too long. Whatever he's getting ready to tell me, it can't be good.

"Your next turn in The Before won't be as Anna," he finally says. "Everyone there will know you as Cassidy Jordan."

"Cassidy," I repeat. The name feels strange on my tongue, and I'm not sure I want to think about the rest of it.

"Your parents will also be second-timers," he continues. "They'll help you with all you need to know for the first six years you're there."

"What happens then?"

"They come back here. A second-timer comes back to The Life-After once their mission is complete. It will look like your parents died in a rock-climbing accident."

A new name, and I get to be an orphan. Fabulous. "What happens to me after that?" I'm not sure I want to hear his other selling points.

"Your aunt and uncle will become your guardians," he answers. "They'll take you to Boston to live with them."

"Will they know what I am?"

"No, and they can't know. That's the first rule of being a second-timer."

It seems like an awfully big secret to keep from your family. "What if I slip up and tell someone?" I ask.

"You won't be able to. If you try to say it, you won't be able to speak. If you try to write it down or type it, your fingers won't be able to move."

"Why don't you want people to know what's next?" It seems to me people would be spared a whole lot of grief if they knew about The Life-After.

"If they did, the purpose of The Before would be gone," he says. "The Before is a phase of working through lower levels of energy, preparing for everything that's here. If people knew what life in The Before really is and what comes next, they would never experience everything required to get here and stay here."

I consider this. I should probably feel overwhelmed, but I still just feel calm. Well, that and creeped out about my new name, new life, and new body.

"Are there other rules?" I ask.

He nods. "The second rule is you have to keep your connection to The Life-After. It will keep your energy up, and you need to have a higher level of energy to stay steady while you're back in The Before."

Energy. This whole thing is like some freaky New Age stuff, so far out there that it doesn't seem possible.

"We're all just energy," he says, his voice sounding gentler now. There he goes, reading my thoughts again. This is all a bit much for me.

"Okay." I pause, looking around me again. I swear the light show is getting brighter. "How do I do that?"

"You have to connect to The Life-After once a day," he replies. "It's kind of like meditating."

Meditation. His answer does nothing to make this seem any less like New-Age-hippie stuff. I turn my head back to him. "When do I go back?"

"Soon."

"What happens if I break one of the rules while I'm there?"

"You won't be able to come back."

"I'll stay in The Before?" I ask. That seems odd. I mean, I know there are books and stuff where fictional people live forever and move around a lot so no one notices, but those books conveniently forget about awesome things like birth certificates and Social Security numbers and all that governments do to keep track of you and make sure you don't escape to some other country in the middle of the night. It's totally unrealistic. Someone would catch on.

It seems like a long time before he answers. "You won't be in The Before, either."

If I'm not in The Before, and I'm not in The Life-After, then that means there's somewhere else. There are more levels to this living stuff than a video game.

"Where will I be?"

"You won't be anywhere," he says. "You won't exist."

I pause. That's not what I expected. It takes me about a minute to decide if this means what I think it does. I have to ask, though. Knowing has to be better than not knowing.

"Is that what happened to David?" My voice is quiet.

"Yes."

That's a little harsh, especially for a place that's all about energy and love. Noah looks at me. Oh right. He heard that.

"Breaking the rules means interfering in someone's fate," he says. "It's what happened to you. The course of your life was changed forever, and David knew it would be. Now you have to go back to The Before because of something he did. There are consequences for that."

I want to argue that it's still harsh, and that it doesn't make sense. I may not have liked my high school science classes all that much, but I paid enough attention to learn that energy can't be created or destroyed. It can only change form. If what he's telling me is true, everything I think I know is wrong.

I'm sure he can hear that thought, too, but he doesn't comment on it. "Why don't I show you around while you're here?" he asks instead. "What you can see of it, anyway."

"Sure."

He gets to his feet and extends a hand to help me up. I let him lead me down a path of shimmering light, deeper into a place I could never have imagined.

The golden light fades until there's only darkness. I open my eyes and blink a few times before reaching over to my bedside table to turn the reading lamp on.

Once my eyes adjust, I grab the newspaper from the table and scan over the articles. There was a time, back when I was Anna, when I read the entertainment section of the Los Angeles Times religiously, along with any other Hollywood news I could get my hands on. Now I usually try to avoid it. I don't recognize many of the names sprinkled across the headlines, and really, I don't care what celebrities are at war with one another this week. I left all of that behind a long time ago.

I do recognize one name on the page, though—Lazy Monday. There's a photo of the band beside the article, which is an announcement for the show they played tonight. The last couple of paragraphs are about band news and an upcoming new album. I yawn, moving my finger to turn the page. Then I see something at the end of the article that makes me stop.

All you fans out there, make sure you get down to the Roxy Theatre on Sunset tomorrow night. For the first time in five years, these guys are playing their favorite old haunt—a special all-ages acoustic show you won't want to miss. If you think that sounds good, it gets even better. Admission is free, but you have to be one of the first 500 people through the door.

I sit up in bed, letting the newspaper fall off my lap and down to the floor. If Riley was at the show tonight, standing that close to the stage, there's a chance he will be at tomorrow's show, too.

"Watch for the signs," I mutter. Maybe there's a reason Noah left the entertainment section open.

"You'll be there, right?" I ask out loud to an imaginary Riley. There's only silence.

I reach over to turn off the reading lamp and then settle back against my pillows, pulling the covers over me. I don't want to think about what happens if Riley doesn't show up at the Roxy tomorrow night.

4

CHAPTER 4

Countdown to The Life-After: seven weeks.

I've never been so thankful for earplugs.

Scratch that. It's intermission I'm thankful for, and it's Riley Davis I'm cursing. As far as I can tell, Mr. Davis didn't have to suffer through the two excruciating warm-up bands that just assaulted my ears. There was no sign of him as I weaved in and out of the crowd during those sets, searching for a glimpse of his too-perfect face.

There wasn't any sign of him in the VIP section, either. Not that I got a good long look at the people sitting there or anything. The beefed-up rent-a-cop in the black T-shirt pounced before I could do more than a quick scan of faces. Standing in the aisle for more than five seconds is a fire hazard, it seems, and he kindly directed me back to the other side of the dividing line. Whatever.

I'm silently cursing Noah, too, for leaving his newspaper open and not bothering to tell me my hunch was all wrong. The Life-After might not be too happy about me cursing him and Riley in my mind, but then, I'm not too happy about the advisor they gave me and all the things he isn't telling me. And let's not even get me started on my feelings about the elusive guy with zero concert etiquette they assigned me to. They can deal with it. Just like I have to deal with being 0-for-2 now, with a few more wasted hours to show for it. Time to bail.

My heels echo against the sidewalk as I walk back in the direction of my car. I study the black cigarette and gum spots that stain the concrete beneath my feet. I don't remember all these spots being here the last time I walked along this part of Sunset Boulevard, years ago. I probably didn't notice then, though, because I was too busy noticing David. This sidewalk is where we met, and that night changed everything.

Honk.

I jump, trying not to fall off the edge of the sidewalk. Some guy in a Prius leans on his horn and hollers out his open window at me, but I can't make out what he says over the noise of the other cars whizzing by. I forgot about this part of walking down Sunset Boulevard at night. Good times.

I cross the street at the next intersection and go down another block, then round the corner onto a side street. It's not as lit up here as it is on Sunset, but it's quieter and that's good enough for me. Or it is until I'm halfway down the street and a wolf-whistle pierces the air.

"Hey, pretty lady," a voice calls out.

Fantastic.

Out of the corner of my eye, I see a few burly men standing in front of an apartment building. So much for leaving the admirers on Sunset. At least these guys don't have a horn to lean on and aren't yelling at the top of their lungs.

I keep walking until I find my path blocked by one of the guys. He reeks of booze and cigarette smoke. I try to twist my lips into a smile, but keep walking. Smiling and saying nothing used to work just fine when I was Anna.

The guy grasps my shoulder, forcing me to stop. His fingertips dig into my skin.

"Where are you off to in such a hurry, beautiful? All the action is that way." With his free hand, he motions in the direction from which I came.

I hold my breath, trying not to inhale the stench coming off him. There's sweat dripping down his forehead, and the look of his eyes tells me he's been doing a lot more than drinking. It takes me a split second to focus and tune into his energy, and I'm careful to keep my energy from connecting with his. The sparks I see surrounding him are weak and almost transparent, even if his physical hold on me is strong. It tells me I need to keep walking.

I gently lift his fingers from my shoulder, leaving him with a polite smile. I get only two steps away before I find myself being spun around. I wince as the guy wrenches my arm.

"No need to be so rude, darlin'. Stay and talk a while."

"I'm meeting someone," I tell him, trying to free myself again. He leers at me, digging his fingers deeper into my skin. My arm will probably bruise, but that's nothing compared with what I could do to him if I wanted to. Energy can be a powerful thing. There are other people watching, though, and I can't risk one of them figuring out there's something different about me. I have a feeling that would be breaking one of the rules.

I open my mouth to speak instead, fighting against what I really want to tell this guy. Running my mouth will only make this get ugly, and fast. Before I can say anything, though, someone else beats me to it.

"She's with me."

I turn my head in the direction of the voice at the same time my friend with the iron grip does. He looks annoyed, but it's all I can do to keep my jaw in place. Riley Davis, it seems, shows up in the strangest places.

The guy holding my arm releases me and takes a step back. "You should teach your girlfriend some manners," he mutters.

Riley raises an eyebrow at him, but he doesn't respond. I look at the guys still standing by the apartment building, wondering if Riley just got us into more trouble than what I was in on my own. They stay where they are, though, and the guy who grabbed my arm takes another few steps away from me.

Riley grabs my hand and pulls me in the other direction without saying a word. A surge of energy shoots through me, and I fight to keep my balance. It's almost impossible to hold my hand steady in his. A tingling feeling spreads through my body, making it hard for me to think.

This has to be an energy drain, somehow caused by the guy who grabbed hold of my arm. I tried hard not to let our energy connect, though, and it doesn't explain why this is happening now that I'm holding Riley's hand. I doubt his energy is at rock-bottom like the other guy's is.

I take a few breaths, trying to clear my mind. We walk for three blocks in silence before I get my bearings and finally find my voice.

"Thank you," I tell him. I swear I hear him snort.

"Yeah, no problem." He sounds put-out and doesn't even try to hide it. If he recognizes me from the concert last night, his face doesn't show it.

We walk a few more steps, then he stops so abruptly that I almost plow into him. He drops my hand.

"Do your parents know you're out roaming the city in the middle of the night?"

His jaw is set, and I'm pretty sure it's irritation I see on his face. Well, this is interesting. I wonder if getting mad at strangers is something he does a lot.

"My parents died when I was six." I regret my words the instant they leave my mouth. Surprise replaces the irritation in his eyes, and then I see exactly what I didn't want to see. He's uncomfortable now. Talking about death seems to do that to people. Discomfort isn't exactly what I was going for, but maybe I shouldn't care. It's better than being lectured.

"I'm sorry." His gaze drops to the sidewalk and stays there.

"Don't be." I start walking again.

"Do you make a habit of walking alone down dark streets at night, this close to bars and people drunk out of their minds?" he calls after me.

Oh, joy. Here we go again.

I stop and turn around. He sounds angry, and a quick check of his energy shows me little red sparks shooting everywhere. Yup, that's definitely the color of anger.

"I got to town a week ago. What am I supposed to do, leave a breadcrumb trail to my house and stay there until new friends magically show up at my door?" I stop talking when something occurs to me. He's out here alone, too. I put my hands on my hips and glare at him. "Why are you giving me a hard time, anyway? I don't see you working the buddy system for safety."

He narrows his eyes. It's completely the wrong time for me to notice they're this incredible shade of deep brown, lit up with little golden flecks here and there. I didn't notice his eyes last night, but they sure have my attention now.

Stop staring, I tell myself. Easier thought than done.

"I'm a little bigger than you," he tells me. I still can't tear my eyes away from him and I think he's noticed, because he's staring right back. I feel warmth run through me and am about to check my energy when I realize energy has nothing to do with it. The heat is in my cheeks. Curse him, I'm blushing.

"And I'm just some weak girl who can't take care of herself?" I challenge, hoping he won't notice my face is turning pink. "That's what you mean, right?"

"I didn't say that."

"You didn't have to. Do you usually lecture complete strangers?"

"Only when I need to rescue them."

"You didn't need to res—" I stop. Arguing with the guy probably won't make my job any easier. I silently count backwards from five and then open my mouth to speak. "Thanks again for helping me, Riley. Most people wouldn't bother." My gaze locks with his and I can feel my face flaming, but at least my voice sounds nice and calm.

He's staring at me again. It takes a second for me to notice that he looks puzzled.

"How do you know my name?" he asks.

5

CHAPTER 5

"Uh." I bite my lip, searching my brain for a reason. I'm about to say he told me his name when I realize I don't have to lie. I open my purse and dig through it, pulling out his student card a few seconds later.

I dangle the card in front of him. "Missing something?"

"Where did you find that?" He reaches out and takes it from my hand.

"On the ground at the Lazy Monday concert we were both at last night. Don't thank me or anything."

"I'm getting attitude from the girl who's roaming the dark streets of L.A. at night?" He glances up at the sky. He's smiling, though, and a quick check of his energy shows me the red sparks are starting to sputter out.

I extend my hand to him. "I'm Cassidy, in case you like to know the names of your damsels in distress once you've delivered them to safety."

He takes my hand. Only a second or two goes by before the tingling starts again. "I guess you already know who I am. For the record, though, I don't really make a habit of giving damsels much attention."

I want to ask what made him stop for me tonight, but the tingling distracts me. It's growing stronger. When I tune into my own energy, I see it's connected with his. Strange. I pull my energy back in toward my body and the tingling stops.

"Not the knight in shining armor type?" I ask, once I can force myself to focus. He shakes his head, releasing my hand. "What made you start with me?"

He shrugs. "You caught me in the right mood, I guess. And you seemed kind of cute and all."

I feel my cheeks getting warm again. "Kind of?" I try to look insulted, but I can tell I'm failing.

A grin spreads across his face. I smile back, since I'm not sure what else to do.

"Where were you coming from, anyway?" he asks. "You look a little young for the bars."

"The Lazy Monday show at the Roxy. Is that where you were?"

"I tried to get in, but the place was full when I got there. I ended up grabbing something to eat at Duke's."

He takes a few steps down the sidewalk, but I don't follow him. "I'm going that way," I call out. When he looks over, I point in the direction opposite from where he's headed. "My car is parked over there."

"Yeah, but I'm parked just past that stop sign, and I'm driving you to your car."

"You don't have to do that." My face still feels hot, although I'm not sure why.

"What kind of knight in shining armor would I be if I let you go back to your car alone?"

I smirk at him. "I thought you weren't a knight in shining armor?"

"I'm not. Are you coming?"

"Yeah, yeah." I walk a little faster to catch up to him.

He opens the passenger door for me when we get to his car, and I slide inside. He gets into the driver's seat a few seconds later. A minute passes before I realize he's not starting the car.

"Is everything okay?" I ask, looking over at him.

He looks thoughtful. "Can I see your phone for a sec?"

"Yeah, sure. Do you need to call someone?" I reach into my purse and pull out my phone. It's strange he's not carrying his phone, given that he wouldn't put it down last night.

He takes the phone from me and starts tapping the screen, then pauses for a few seconds.

"Need help using it?" I ask.

He shakes his head and starts to type something. When he finishes, he hands the phone back to me.

"I don't know," he says. "You tell me."

I look down and see a new entry in my contacts list. Riley Davis. Call for emergencies. His number is below that.

"Call for emergencies?" I ask.

He starts the car. "You said you're new here. You need someone you can call if something happens."

For someone who doesn't want to rescue strangers, he sure seems concerned about my safety. I'd point this out to him, but something tells me not to push it.

"Thanks," I say instead, slipping my phone back into my purse.

"No problem. Where'd you say your car was?" He glances at the rear-view mirror and then pulls out onto the street.

"It's over on Melrose."

The only talking I do for the rest of the short ride is to give directions. It's not long before we pull up to the curb behind my car.

"Thanks," I tell him. I wonder if I should hug him or something.

Since when do you hug anyone? I remind myself. It must be the energy surges messing with my mind. I reach for the door handle.

"Drive safely," he says. "And be safe."

I look back at him and smile, then get out of the car.

He stays parked behind me until I'm inside my own car. Once I'm in the driver's seat, gripping the steering wheel, I notice my hands are shaking. When Riley pulls away from the curb and passes me, I drop them to my lap so he can't see that I'm trembling.

I've found him again, and I even have a way of reaching him now, but I'm still in the dark about what comes next. I always thought when I found the person I was sent here to help, everything I needed to do would become obvious. After that, getting back to The Life-After would be a piece of cake. Unless I have some kind of epiphany in my sleep tonight, it's clear I was wrong. If I don't figure this out soon, I'll fail both of us.

This is the only chance I'll get. I just wish I knew where to begin.

The little orange light on my phone is blinking when I get home and walk into the kitchen. I set my purse down on the counter and scan through the call log. The only entry there is my aunt and uncle's home phone number, a call I must have missed by just a few minutes after leaving for the Lazy Monday show. It was still evening here, but considering the time difference, it was pretty late for anyone to be calling me from Boston.

I pick up the phone and press the voicemail button. My uncle's voice comes through the speaker.

"Hi Cassidy, it's Uncle Mike. Call me back when you can. There's a letter here for you from Harvard. Your aunt opened it in case it was important, and it's a good thing she did. There's been some kind of mix-up with the admissions office since they seem to think you won't be starting classes in the fall. We should get this straightened out first thing Monday morning."

I hold the phone out in front of me, listening to the beep when the message ends. There are a few choice words I could use right now, but none of them would come close to being the right one for this.

I wasn't counting on a follow-up letter from Harvard, or at least not this soon. The information in the letter isn't wrong. The mistake is my aunt and uncle finding out I have no plans to start college in a few weeks, and it's a big one.

At least it's the middle of the night in Boston. That gives me some time to figure out my story, since I definitely can't tell them the truth.

6

CHAPTER 6

I push open the door of Amoeba Records and walk inside, coming to a dead stop three steps past the entrance. I was just looking for a decent indie record store when I found this place listed online, but this is more like some kind of music palace. There's way more vinyl than anywhere I used to sneak off to in Boston. Holy cow. This could take me all day.

Some guy who clearly knows where he's going brushes past me. Oh right. I'm blocking the door. I take a few more steps into the store, and then spot the signs hanging from the ceiling. Okay, good. I can find things here kind of like I can at the grocery store. I scan the signs until I see one for the rock section and head in that direction, breathing in the scent of the plastic album sleeves. It might be the best smell that exists in The Before. Not quite The Life-After, but this will do for a couple of hours.

I stop in front of one of the shelves, and then turn around to see what else is behind me. That's when a blond head one row over catches my eye. There's only one person standing in that row, and his hair looks mighty familiar. Hmmm.

I tiptoe closer, watching as the guy I've spotted plucks an album out from one of the racks to examine the cover. It's definitely Riley, unless he has a twin brother. I try to get a closer look at the album in his hands, and then have to smother a laugh when I realize what he's holding. I wouldn't have pegged him for a fan of Top 40 tween pop.

I take a step toward him, thinking about appearing at his side and teasing him about what his favorite song on the album is. Then I stop, another thought crossing my mind. I can have way more fun with this.

I quietly move to stand by a nearby wall, concealing myself behind a rack of magazines. After I dig my phone out of my purse, I find the number he gave me last night and tap out a text message.

It's Cassidy. You said to get in touch if there's an emergency, and there's definitely an emergency. Send. I hear a quiet chiming sound a second later.

I watch him put the album down and reach into his pocket to pull out his phone. He glances at the screen and frowns, then starts typing. I look down at my phone to make sure I have the sound turned off.

His message appears on my screen a second later. Where are you? Are you okay?

I clamp a hand over my mouth to keep from laughing out loud. Once I'm sure I have it under control, I remove my hand and type a reply.

I'm fine. Your taste in music might need a 911 call, though. I send the message and look over at him, waiting to see his face when he reads it.

His phone chimes again and he raises it closer to his face to see the screen. He jerks his head to the left and then to the right, squinting when he looks at the far end of the store.

"Behind you," I say, stepping out from my hiding spot by the magazine rack. He turns around. I can't keep the grin off of my face when he shoots me a dark look.

"Not funny. I thought you were in trouble."

"Nope. I'm here to rescue you this time, from your tragic taste in music." I point at the album he's put down. "Tweeny girl pop on vinyl? Here I had you as more of an alt-indie kind of guy."

"It's for my niece." I can tell he's trying to keep a sour expression, but the corners of his lips twitch up into a smile.

"Well then, she's lucky to have an uncle who'd risk being spotted with that. It could ruin a guy, you know."

"Impressed now, are you?" he asks. I can see he's trying not to laugh.

"Don't let it go to your head."

"I wouldn't dream of it." He slings his arm around my shoulder, turning me in the direction of the cash register at the front of the store. Just like last night, a tingling feeling spreads through me at his touch. It makes me dizzy.

Once he pays for the album, he steers me out of the store. I'm not really sure where we're going, but he's not telling me adios or anything, so I go with it.

"That was rude, you know," I tell him.

"What was?"

"Cutting my shopping trip short. You didn't even ask if I was finished looking around." He looks at me, probably to see if I'm serious. The expression on his face makes it impossible not to laugh.

"Damsel in distress one night, and a sarcastic pain in the you-know-what less than twenty-four hours later," he mutters. "How exactly do I keep running into you?"

"You're just one incredibly lucky guy." I punch him lightly on the shoulder, and I swear I hear him grunt.

"Lucky isn't really the word I'd use." He tries to sound grumpy, but I can tell he's amused. He seems more relaxed than last night, anyway.

"How old is your niece?" I ask, letting him lead me down the street.

"She'll be seven soon." I can tell from the look on his face that he adores her.

"How are you old enough to have a seven-year-old niece?"

"Maybe I'm actually fifty." He arches an eyebrow at me.

"Maybe your student card told me your real age." I arch an eyebrow back at him. I already know he turned nineteen last month. "So back to my question."

"I'm the baby in the family, and my niece is my older sister's daughter. Want to grab lunch with me?" He stops walking, so I do, too. I look up and see we're standing beside the patio of a café.

"Eating is always good. What is this place?"

He puts his hands on my shoulders, turning me toward the door. "It's my secret hideaway. Best panini in Hollywood."

The interior of the café looks like it could be someone's house circa the 1950s, except for the deli case and antique cash register. I follow Riley to the counter, noticing the worn look of the dark wood surface.

He takes a menu from a holder on the counter and hands it to me. I open it, but have to strain to read the tiny print on the page. For such a small place, the sandwich selection is almost ridiculously big.

"The apple one," he says.

"Hmm?" I shift my gaze up to him.

"The panini with apples and brie." He points at the middle of the menu. "You can't go wrong if you like apples, or even if you think you don't."

"You like apples, I take it?" I wonder if he knows how earnest his face is right now. Probably not.

"I'm a guy. I like pretty much anything."

"Ha. Very true." I read the description and have to admit it sounds good. I'll get it, but not because he suggested it.

"What do you want to drink?"

"Whatever's on tap," I say. He looks me up and down, frowning. I can tell he's trying to decide if I'm joking.

"Are you even old enough to drink?" he finally asks. "You look like you're sixteen."

"I'm seventeen, actually. Eighteen on Saturday."

"And still not even close to being old enough to order drinks," he finishes without missing a beat. "Neither am I, for that matter."

"You're no fun at all, are you?" I pretend to make a face at him and he chuckles.

"Why do I get the feeling you're kind of a handful?" I can't deny that, but he doesn't need to know. Before I can come up with a good answer, the cashier finishes with the person in front of us and asks to take our order. I get the apple and brie panini and an iced tea, and Riley orders the same thing.

"Copycat," I tell him.

"Great minds think alike." He takes a wire stand with our order number on it from the cashier, and then we head outside to the patio. Our iced teas are brought over by a waiter almost as soon as we sit down.

"So, eighteen this weekend," Riley muses, leaning back in his chair. "You must have big plans for celebrating?"

"Nope." I take a sip of my iced tea.

"So that means your family is coming to town and you're keeping it tame."

He's teasing me, but he wouldn't be if he knew my family. "Nope," I say again.

I can tell he wants to ask me another question. It's time to make something up before he can start digging.

7

CHAPTER 7

"**M**y aunt and uncle can't get away from Boston this weekend because of some family thing going on there," I lie. "I just didn't want to go back for it."

"Your aunt and uncle?" He looks confused for a second, then he shifts his eyes away from me. Yup. He remembers now. "Do you miss your parents on your birthday?"

I take another sip of my drink while thinking about how to answer him. I have to be careful with this, since it's clear death isn't a subject he's comfortable with. Not that I can blame him, really. It's the same for most people. I release my straw from my lips.

"My parents are always here with me, celebrating my life from above." My voice is gentle, but his cheeks still flush.

"You had to miss them growing up, though, didn't you?" he asks after a moment.

"I loved them growing up, or at least my memory of them." I watch him swallow, even though he hasn't taken a sip from his glass. He looks away from me again, focusing on something I can't see on the sidewalk. Fail. We've veered straight into awkward.

I try to think of a way to change the subject, but he turns his head back to me and speaks before I can.

"If you're not doing anything for your birthday, I'll take you out."

Like on a date? I freeze as the thought pops into my mind. I don't date, or at least I haven't since I was Anna. It just doesn't make sense to let anyone get attached to me. It makes even less sense now, since I won't be here in a couple of months.

I'm about to answer him when I realize he's still talking. "You have to celebrate your birthday. You know that, right?" Looks like Riley is one of those persistent people. Super.

I set my elbow on the table, propping my head up with my hand. I'm not sure there's a way out of this one. If I'm here to help him with something, that probably means I have to spend time with him. It would just help if we didn't spend that time on something that sounds like a date.

"I'm over birthdays," I finally say. I'm not sure if this answers his question or not.

Apparently not. "You're too young to be over birthdays," he informs me. Great.

Our food shows up before I can come up with a good argument for that. Riley reaches for his sandwich but keeps looking at me. His eyes dare me to challenge him.

"Wisdom of the ancient one?" I finally offer. I catch him mid-bite, and he can only smirk until he swallows his mouthful of food.

"Are you always this sarcastic?"

"I usually save it for family." I give him my most innocent look.

"I'm flattered."

"You should be," I agree. I pick up my panini and take a bite.

If I add up the years of life I've had in The Before as both Anna and Cassidy, I'm more than justified in my feelings about birthdays. This isn't something I can explain to Riley, though.

"Think about where you want to go on Saturday," he says. I can tell he's not great at taking no for an answer. Well, we sure have that in common.

"Won't your girlfriend be jealous?" I ask. It's a joke, but there's an odd look creeping across Riley's face. It tells me that was a bad choice of words. Interesting.

He looks away from me and lifts his glass to his lips. After taking a drink, he sets it back down on the table.

"I'm not really a girlfriend kind of guy."

He gets really quiet, then. Even though most people are quiet when they eat, this feels more uncomfortable than when we were talking about death. Someone has to break the silence here, and clearly it's going to be me.

"Was that the wrong thing to bring up?" I reach for my fork so I can spear a cucumber from my side salad.

He blinks a couple of times before my words register. "No."

He's lying. He knows I can tell, or I think he does, because he opens his mouth to speak again.

"I live inside of my head sometimes."

"Me too." I go for a tomato this time.

"You're seventeen. Get out of your head."

I make a face at him. "You're nineteen, lead by example."

He laughs, picking his glass up again. "What's that old saying? 'Do as I say, not as I do'?"

"I think we just call that hypocrisy in Boston."

"Consider me schooled."

He's studying me, I notice. I pretend to be occupied with eating my salad. When I've taken a few bites and see he's still watching me, I can't pretend to ignore him anymore.

"What?"

He grins at the impatience in my voice. "Just curious what brought you out here."

"Life." I put my fork down.

"Let me guess. You're an actress?"

I try not to choke as a mouthful of iced tea slides down my throat. No, but I was in my last life. There's something I sure can't say out loud. I shake my head after a moment.

"Model?" he tries again.

This time I do choke on my iced tea, but it's because I'm laughing. I reach for my napkin and hold it over my mouth while I cough a couple of times, putting it back down on the table when I think I've recovered. At least the iced tea didn't come out my nose.

"Maybe when my long-anticipated six-inch growth spurt happens, but I'm not holding my breath," I tell him. "I'm a little too short for the model life, if you haven't noticed."

"It was a compliment, actually. You don't take those well, do you?"

I feel my cheeks getting warm. He must notice it too, because I see glee in his eyes. He's found the weakness in my armor and he knows it.

"Fashion school?" he guesses. Now he's just goading me.

"I was supposed to be starting my first year of pre-med at Harvard this fall. They accepted me, but I changed my mind and canceled on them."

He whistles. "How'd that go over with your family?"

"They don't know yet." Well, they kind of don't know. I haven't called my uncle back.

"But they know you moved to L.A.?" He looks confused.

"They think I'm here for summer vacation and that I'm going back to Boston before the fall semester starts."

"What happens when you tell them the truth?"

"I'm still figuring that out," I lie. As long as I can convince them I've called the admissions office and sorted everything out, I won't need to tell them anything.

He takes another bite of his food, and the silence is a relief. The guy is a question-asking machine. No one has ever gotten this much information about my life out of me, and I can't say I like it too much. He swallows. I get ready for the next question.

"Boston is a long way from here. Why'd you choose L.A.?"

I shrug and stab my fork into a piece of lettuce. "I needed some time out, and I wanted to figure out who I am away from everything and everyone I grew up with. Maybe it's my quarter-life crisis." It sounds like a good enough excuse to me.

"You're at least a few years away from your quarter-life crisis." And now I know he can do math in his head, too.

"What can I say? I'm mature for my age." I watch him take a bite of his salad. Perfect. It's time to turn the focus back to him while his mouth is too full of food to ask me another question. "Where'd you learn how to interrogate people, anyway?"

He swallows and wipes his mouth with his napkin. "A year of journalism school," he answers. "Come talk to me after the next three years."

"Ah, so that's what you're taking at USC."

"That, and a double major in English. Why have one major when you can kill your social life with two?"

"And then you'll be cross-examining politicians and people on the street?"

"Maybe," he shrugs. "I really just want to write books."

"Are you writing a book?"

"Yep." He takes another bite of his panini and we spend the next few minutes in silence, finishing our food. Once the last crumbs have disappeared from our plates, he checks his watch.

"I need to head out soon," he says, looking up at me. "Work to do."

I nod, setting my napkin down on the table. "Thanks for lunch."

He leaves a few bills on the table for our waiter, and then we both get up from our chairs. He follows me through the patio exit and out onto the sidewalk. We start to walk back in the direction of the record store.

"Do you live around here?" he asks.

"Kind of. I'm up in the Hills."

"Ah, so you're a rich kid. I guess the Harvard thing should have clued me in."

"Yeah, because I hear the University of Southern California is the main hangout of the nation's paupers. Don't they call it the University of Spoiled Children, or is that another USC?" I actually want to stick my tongue out at him, but my almost-eighteen-year-old self wins out over the six-year-old in me.

"You're way too fun to tease, you know."

I roll my eyes at him. Okay, so the six-year-old in me hasn't entirely lost the battle.

"The house I live in has been in my family for practically forever," I tell him.

"Do you live there all by yourself?"

I'm about to joke that it's just a bunch of ghosts and me, but then I remember that the last couple of times I've mentioned dead people haven't gone over so well. If we're going to hang out, I have to figure out some way to get him over this.

"Just me," I answer. Amoeba Music is only a few steps away now. We stop at the corner, and I wonder if he's going to walk me all the way to my car. He checks his watch again.

"Time for me to jet, or I'll be late for work. I meant what I said, though, about your birthday. Let me take you out to celebrate."

Oh right. Guess he's one of those people with a good memory, too. Fabulous.

"Um, sure," I reply. Maybe something brilliant will come to me when I get home and we can cancel. Then I can figure out a way to see him again without the words "take you out" being part of it.

"I'll text you later this week," he says. Wonderful.

"Until then." I lift my hand and wriggle my fingers at him. He touches my shoulder and I feel the tingling again. It stops when he drops his hand and turns to walk in the other direction.

I'm still a little light-headed when I get to my car, even though the tingling is gone. Once I'm sitting inside, I lean my head against the back of the seat and wait for the feeling to pass. That's when a flash of white on the passenger seat catches my eye. There's a long white feather resting there. I can guess how it got in here, but I know it's not from Noah. He only sends me indigo feathers.

I wrack my brain, trying to figure out who else could be sending me a feather, and why. My mind draws a complete blank. I must be forgetting someone, but I'm sure it will come to me. I open the glove compartment and put the feather inside, then start my car and pull away from the curb.

8

CHAPTER 8

Countdown to The Life-After: six weeks.

I try not to shiver when the marker squeaks against the page. One line, and then another. X. It's my favorite sight.

I've crossed off days on a calendar since I was six years old, starting right after my parents died. A calendar was the only thing I asked for the first time my aunt and uncle took me to the biggest toy store I'd ever seen, right after I came to live with them in Boston. They were surprised, and I couldn't blame them, really. What kid asks for a calendar? Most six-year-olds probably would have asked for a pony.

Uncle Mike likes the idea of crossing off days gone by, probably because he thinks I'm counting down the days until I start college. He's right about me counting down, just not about what I'm counting down to. I've never told him he's wrong, though. It's easier to let him and Aunt Sarah believe what they need to. It keeps the peace.

I set the marker down on the kitchen counter. The next uncrossed box on the calendar is for today, my eighteenth birthday. I always thought today would feel like freedom in a way, since it's the last birthday I'll celebrate as Cassidy. Freedom isn't what I feel, though. Not right now, just a couple of hours from the date I've been forced into going on. If that's even what this birthday dinner with Riley is, since it's hard to tell what he has in mind. I'm hoping it's just a pity dinner, and that he insisted on taking me out because he thinks I'm all alone out here in the big, bad city. I could live with that. A pity dinner means no expectations and no mess to clean up later.

It's not that I haven't gone out on dates before. I just wasn't Cassidy the last time I did, and I kind of wanted to keep it that way. Dating as Anna wasn't dangerous for anyone but me. Dating now definitely is. It's a bad idea to let someone get close when I know how much it will hurt them once I'm gone.

I look at the clock on the stove. It's five-thirty, which means I have an hour and a half to get ready. Curse everyone, and especially David Burns. I should be in The Life-After right now, not walking into a complete disaster.

"Do what you gotta do," I mutter, picking up my phone from the counter. Then I head for the bathroom to take a shower.

The doorbell rings at 7 o'clock sharp. Awesome. Not only is Riley a reluctant rescuer who just can't leave things alone, he's also uber-punctual. I try to plaster something that looks like cheer on my face and then reach for the handle of the front door.

"Hi." It's the only word I get out before noticing the bouquet of roses in his hand. My mouth clamps shut. This is my worst nightmare.

"Hey, birthday girl," he says, taking a step forward and reaching his arms out to give me a hug. I can't remember the last time I hugged somebody, and my arms feel like alien tentacles. I'm sure my face is flaming.

He releases me and holds out the bouquet. "Not the most original birthday gift, I know."

I take it from him, twisting my lips into something I hope looks like a smile. "Being a gentleman today, are you?" I should just thank him, I know. I don't.

"I'll deny it if anyone ever asks." His gaze is glued to me, I notice, and I quickly drop mine to stare at the flowers. "You look incredible," he adds.

Yup. My face is on fire. "Thanks. Um, let me go put these in something." We're two minutes into this night and I already need an escape. The nightmare is getting worse.

He follows me inside, waiting in the foyer by the front door while I head to the kitchen to deal with the flowers. I don't have a vase, so I put them in the first pitcher I can find and fill it with water. This can only go downhill from here.

This is my job, I remind myself, taking a few deep breaths. Then I'm dragging my feet back out of the kitchen and down the hall to where I left Riley.

"Ready?" I ask. There. That at least sounded like I'm not dreading this more than the conversation about Harvard I still have to have with my uncle and aunt, even though I am.

"After you." He holds open the door, his eyes following me when I pass by him. He's still watching me when I lock the deadbolt and walk ahead of him to the car.

There's a white feather on the driveway right beside Riley's car. It looks almost identical to the one I found after we had lunch the other day, only I know that one is still in my glove compartment. I stop for a moment, not sure if I should leave it there or pick it up. Riley must take this as his cue that I'm waiting for him to be all chivalrous or something, because he appears at my side and opens the passenger door before I can recover and reach for it myself. Terrific. Now we're definitely acting like this is a date. Damn feather.

"Thanks." I duck inside of the car. He closes my door and gets into the driver's seat a moment later. Silence. Well, this is awkward.

Sitting this close to him, I can feel the tingling again. My body sways. I grab hold of the handle on the door and sit up straight in the seat.

"Where are we going tonight?" I ask, fighting to clear the haze from my mind.

He shrugs and then winks at me. Okay, seriously. Who does that?

He won't tell me where we're going until we pull into the parking garage at The Grove. I know it's home to a bunch of stores and restaurants, but I've never been here before. It wasn't built yet when I was Anna.

I know I'm in deep trouble the second we step off the escalator. Walking into The Grove is like strolling into a fairytale, complete with cobblestones and a trolley. There's even a fountain in the middle of it all with jumping streams of water. Gorgeous? Yes. And so in-your-face romantic that I have to look away. It's exactly the kind of place a guy takes a girl on a date, and it's probably not where you go for a pity dinner. This is bad.

We stop at the entrance to the patio of a restaurant called La Piazza. I normally love Italian food, but I already know I like it better when I'm eating alone, watching TV. Riley talks to the host while I have another look around. The restaurant's patio overlooks the fountain and its footbridge. I try not to groan. The view is nice and all, but I can't help wishing we were some place on Sunset Boulevard right now, yelling at each other over a horrible band. Better still, it would be so loud that we wouldn't be able to talk to each other at all. Why did I let him plan this?

I feel Riley nudge me. "After you, ma'am," he whispers into my ear. I turn my head back to face him and see that our host is waiting for us, holding two menus in his hand. Well, we're here. Let's get this over with.

I follow the host, Riley trailing right behind me. "Eighteen years old and already a ma'am," I say, glancing back over my shoulder. "That came fast."

"I thought you'd appreciate it more than 'missy'."

"You've got that right."

I stop at the table the host is standing beside. We're on the edge of the patio, only a few feet from the fountain. The host makes a move to pull out my chair for me, but Riley beats him to it. The continuation of date manners. This is more than bad.

Riley sits down across the table from me. I fiddle with my napkin and pretend to watch the fountain until a waiter comes by with a basket of bread and asks to take our drink order. My eyes accidentally meet Riley's when I order an iced tea, which is exactly what I was trying not to do. Eye contact means conversation, and date conversation means that awful small talk people are forced to have in situations exactly like this one. It doesn't matter that we had a completely normal and easy conversation just a few days ago. It never does when you go on a date.

"So, how'd you spend the rest of your big day?" he asks, once the waiter leaves our table.

There it is. I watch the waiter disappear inside and force myself to move my eyes back to Riley. He unfolds his napkin, waiting for me to answer.

"Big day?" I repeat. I know what he means, but he sounds so formal and like he's seventy or something. Who even asks that unless they're on a date, trying to force some kind of horrifying conversation? He should have made this a pity dinner.

"Your birthday. Did you have a good day?"

I kind of want to grab his shoulders and shake him a little bit. I reach for the breadbasket instead.

"It was relaxing," I tell him. "I went for a swim and then read by my pool for a while."

"Reading anything good?"

I'm not about to tell him I was reading a trashy romance novel I picked up at the airport in Boston before my flight out here. "Yeah. It's something about string theory," I lie.

String theory? I have no idea where that came from, but that's what dates do to me.

He stops with his fork halfway to his mouth. "String theory?"

Does he really have to pay attention to what I say? Geez.

"Mmm-hmm." I pray he doesn't ask me to explain it to him. I'd fail spectacularly.

"Not a romance novel kind of girl?" He reaches for his water glass but seems unable to move his eyes away from me. I feel little electrical currents dance across my skin. When I focus, I see his energy pushing into mine.

"What?" I ask him, when he continues to stare. "Are you afraid of a girl with a brain?" He needs to ease up or I'm going to be jolted out of my chair.

He looks down at his plate. I let out a breath when his energy backs off. "It's actually kind of sexy," he says. Or I think he says it, since he's looking down and mumbling.

My breath catches in my throat. That's not what I expected him to say, and I have no idea how to answer him.

9

CHAPTER 9

I need to get myself back together, which means breathing normally again. While I figure out how to do this, I buy myself some time by pretending to find smoothing out my napkin absolutely fascinating.

"Did I say the wrong thing?" he asks, after a few seconds of silence.

"Hmm? No." I force myself to look up at him. I can tell he isn't convinced.

"You have the tiniest little frown on your face right now," he says.

"Oh. Really?" I hadn't noticed any muscles in my face moving. The tingling is making it hard to notice much of anything.

"Yeah. I don't think most people would have noticed it, but—" He stops and looks down at his plate, his cheeks turning the color of tomatoes. I sense we're headed straight back to small talk, so it may as well be me who starts it this time.

"Do you want the last slice of bread?" I ask. He looks up, but he's not looking at me.

"It's all yours."

Both of us decide at the same moment that it's a good time to look at the menu. It takes care of conversation for a couple of minutes, anyway. Once I decide on what I'm having, I fold the menu up and set it on the table, turning my head to look out at the courtyard. Streams of water shoot high up into the air from the fountain, the lights making the leaping water look almost like shooting stars. Talk about way too obviously romantic.

Our waiter comes to take our order almost the second Riley puts his menu down and then there we are, back to figuring out what to say. I think for a moment and then grab on to the first thing that comes to mind.

"Did your niece like the record?" His face brightens. I try not to sigh with relief.

"She told me I'm still her favorite uncle when she saw it," he says. It's not hard to tell this kid has him wrapped around her finger. She probably knows it, too. I kind of wish I knew what it was like to have a niece, but I never will.

Dinner gets easier after that, somehow, or at least it does if I'm going by the fact that I no longer want to shake him. He tells me about his job at his parents' recording studio, and about the first time he saw Lazy Monday play. Whenever the conversation turns to my life, I find a way to steer it back to him. Nice try, but there's no chance I'm going to tell him anything more than he already knows. He learned enough about me at lunch a few days ago.

After dinner, we walk through The Grove and the Farmers Market next door, until the shops and stalls start shutting down and we decide to leave. Our fingers brush by accident when we turn around to head back to his car, and for just a second, I think he might take my hand in his. The second passes, though, and he shoves his hands into his pockets. I fumble with my purse, pretending to look for a stick of gum. We walk the rest of the way to the parking garage with about a foot of space between us. Yup, we've gone straight back to awkward. Dates are never a good idea.

The radio saves us when Riley starts the car. The song playing is just begging for me to make fun of it.

"Folk?" I eye him as he pulls out of our parking spot. "Let's try a rock station, maybe?"

He smirks. "It's on a rock station."

"What, did the music director blow out his eardrums at too many real rock shows?"

"Banjos are the new guitar solo. What cave have you been living in?"

"One with much better stations than this." I lunge for the radio and change the station.

"Keep going," he warns me. "There's no dubstep allowed in this car."

"Yet you allow indie folk and call it rock." I pretend to sigh. "This is a sad day for our friendship."

"Guess I won't be giving you my extra ticket to Bon Iver." He turns out of the garage and onto the street.

"I have to wash my hair that night, anyway."

"You don't even know what night it is."

"It doesn't matter."

He grins, keeping his eyes on the road. I take the opportunity to study him from out of the corner of my eye while pretending to look at something on my phone. When I focus, I can see that our energy is joined together, which doesn't surprise me since I'm tingling again. Little golden sparkles light up the space where our energy meets. The sparkles get bigger and multiply, and the tingling feeling grows stronger. It's hard to think or speak, so I turn up the radio and we listen to the music blasting through the speakers for the rest of the drive.

I expect to say a quick goodbye in the car after we pull into my driveway, but Riley parks the car and gets out to come open my door. Ah, yes. The walk to the front porch. I know how this walk after a date used to end for me when I was Anna. I also know kissing the person I'm here to help is a really bad idea.

The logical part of my brain doesn't seem to be communicating with the rest of me, though. It's as though I'm under a spell as I put one foot in front of the other, feeling Riley's hand pressed against the small of my back. My body is going crazy with the tingling I feel. I must stumble, because he steadies me and we stop a few feet away from my front door. I find myself moving even closer to him, and for a moment, I'm not Cassidy. There's something familiar in the energy I feel. Riley's face blurs in front of me, and then there's the outline of a face I used to know well.

The outline I can see looks like David. The last time I stood in a driveway about to kiss someone, it was him. I want to say his name, but I can't move my lips. Then my vision clears and it's Riley in front of me again, his head bending down and his eyes holding mine. The energy pull between us is magnetic, and I hold my breath when his fingertips come up to my chin.

This can't happen. I try to tell myself that, but the rest of me isn't listening. My eyes close and every nerve in my body seems to hum as I wait for what's coming. I'm going to regret this kiss the second it happens. Then there's nothing, save for the stroke of a thumb tip across my cheek. My eyes open just in time to see Riley take a step back, his hand dropping to his side like he wasn't just mere seconds away from brushing my lips with his. He's standing so straight now, his arms so stiff, I almost think I imagined what just happened. I should be relieved, though. No, make that ecstatic. I can't say either feeling has hit me yet.

"Do you want to come in for a few minutes?" The words tumble from my mouth before I can stop them, and they don't feel like mine.

Riley's mouth curves into a small smile. There's an expression on his face I can't read, and I see him shake his head. "It's late. I think we should both get some sleep."

That's when I notice the tingling is fading. The energy around us has changed. I focus and see that Riley's energy is pulled in close around him. The colors are different now, and I can tell something has his guard up. That's a little weird. There's nothing to be afraid of here, since we're probably in the safest neighborhood in L.A.

"Okay," I say. "Goodnight, then?"

He touches my shoulder. His fingers rest there for no more than a second, but it's long enough for me to feel a tremor in his hand.

"Goodnight," he replies.

I should be grateful this is how the night is ending, because a goodnight kiss would be a mistake. Instead, I'm confused about his shaking fingers and about why his energy closes in even more tightly around him when he walks down the driveway to his car and gets inside.

I turn around before he can see me watching him and hurry to open the front door. I don't know if he's even out of the driveway yet when I close the door behind me and lean against it, feeling short of breath.

My legs crumple beneath me and I feel myself hit the floor. Everything goes black.

10

CHAPTER 10

"Welcome back."

Everything in front of me is blurry when I open my eyes. It takes a few seconds for the room to come into focus. I'm in the foyer, lying on the floor. Noah is kneeling beside me.

I push myself into a sitting position, maybe a little too fast. My body pitches to the side and my head comes dangerously close to the floor again, my blood seeming to rush up to my temples all at once. Noah's arm shoots out to steady me.

"What happened?" I croak, letting him pull me back up. My skin feels clammy.

"Funny you should ask."

I don't see how there could be anything funny about blacking out and finding myself on the floor. My brain and my voice aren't cooperating too well, though, and it feels like way too much work to tell him this.

"Why don't we get you outside for some air?" he suggests. "That might help."

I nod and let him help me to my feet, swaying a little as I stand. He waits until he's sure I have my balance and then leads me down the hall and through the living room, outside to the balcony. I sit down on the loveseat, stretching out and leaning my head against the cushions. That's better. It feels less like the world is spinning. Noah takes the chair across from me.

I breathe in the cool air, looking past Noah and out into the darkened sky. I haven't seen stars since leaving Boston, since the city lights here block out almost everything but the moon. But there's a place just outside of the city where it's dark enough to see thousands or maybe even millions of stars and the trails of stardust in between them. It was my favorite place to go when I was Anna. I haven't been back since then.

"How are you feeling?" Noah asks.

I squeeze my eyes shut against the dull throbbing in my head. "Not like I could leap a tall building or anything, but better. My head hurts a little."

"It will for a while. That happens when your energy gets that weak."

So that's what this is all about. Nobody ever told me weak energy could make me pass out. I open my eyes and look at Noah.

"How did my energy get that low?" I ask.

"From connecting with Riley's energy. That's my best guess, anyway." He stretches his legs out in front of him, shifting down in the chair. Great, he's getting comfortable. It looks like this conversation is going to take a while.

"Is that supposed to happen?"

"It can. His energy has more of a pull on you than anyone else you've spent time with in The Before, because you're here to help him. You just connect that way. You'll give him as much energy as he needs, but his energy is naturally lower than yours since he's not a second-timer. That means when your energy connects with his and you make his energy stronger, your energy gets weaker."

"And you couldn't have told me this before I went out with him tonight?" It's not like Noah has had eighteen years to mention it or anything. No big deal.

He ignores the sarcasm in my voice. "I didn't know your energy would get this weak, or that it would happen so fast. The way you connect to The Life-After to level out your energy might not be enough for you anymore."

I squint at him. Unless there's something he hasn't explained how to do over the years, I'm pretty sure I have zero control over how I connect. The Life-After takes care of that part. Maybe he means how often I do it.

"You want me to connect more than once a day?" I ask.

"I want you to connect a little more strongly."

"Do you mean you want me to stay connected for longer?" I can't see how I'd do that, either, since I just get disconnected when my energy is where it needs to be.

He shakes his head. "There's someone I want you to see who can help. Her name is Amarleen."

"Is she another advisor?" I ask. Let's hope not. Two wardens is exactly what I don't need.

"She's a teacher at Diamond Lotus Yoga. I want you to join her class."

I watch his face. If he's pulling my leg, then he's an even better actor than I was when I was Anna.

"You want me to go to a yoga class to make my energy stronger?" I ask the question slowly, trying to make sure he means what I think he does. "Like hot rooms crammed with people in spandex, sweating it out to downward dog and trying to out-leg-lift the person beside them while they pretend to be one with the world?" My eyebrows are so high, I'm surprised they haven't shot off my forehead.

He chuckles. "It's not the kind of yoga you're thinking of. You'll understand when you get there."

"Whatever you say." I think it would be easier if I just had a way of not letting Riley's energy connect with mine, or at least not as strongly. What do I know, though?

"That won't work," Noah answers. I guess he heard that. "You can't avoid this, even though you want to."

I bite down on the inside of my lip, trying to squash the words I can feel on the tip of my tongue. I'm too tired to have this argument with him right now.

Noah told me once that the last weeks of my life as Anna imprinted on my energy and left a dead spot there that I still carry with me. I know it's there because I can see the spot he means, just over my heart. It's like a scar, always without sparks of color. He thinks what caused the scar also makes me avoid getting close enough to someone for our energy to connect, and that I'm protecting myself. He won't believe I'm trying to protect other people from missing me when I'm gone.

"Okay," I tell him. I'll keep the peace tonight. He looks satisfied with my answer, for now at least.

"I think you should go connect for a while now, and then try to get some sleep." It's more than a thought, though. He has that stern-college-professor tone in his voice, which makes it a command. I used to think he was a teacher during his time in The Before, but then I asked him about his life there. He told me he was his village's matchmaker, and I still haven't figured out if he was kidding or not. Noah has never really struck me as the lovey-dovey romantic type.

I watch him get up from his chair. He's about to leave, I know, but there's something else on my mind. I open my mouth and then pause, closing it again. Maybe bringing this up isn't such a good idea.

"You have a question for me?" Too late. Either he was watching me, or he heard my thoughts. I'd bet good money he already knows what I'm going to ask.

"I thought I saw David's energy tonight," I tell him.

It's so quiet, I can hear the breeze rustling the trees. Noah turns his back to me and walks over to the balcony railing. I can't see his face when he speaks.

"You know nothing of David exists anymore." There's the stern professor voice again.

"I know." I don't, but I should have known this would be his answer.

"Is that all?" He still has his back to me. I look past him, out at the city skyline.

"No. I'd like to know what Riley needs help with."

"You'll figure it out soon enough."

I try not to roll my eyes. "You're impossible. You know that, don't you?"

He turns away from the railing and tips his fedora at me. I can tell it's the end of our conversation for tonight.

"Just doing my job," he says. "Sleep well tonight." Then he's gone.

I rest my head against the back of the loveseat, listening to the crickets chirp from somewhere below. Noah always leaves me with more questions than answers. One day soon, I'm going to run out of time to figure the answers out on my own.

11

CHAPTER 11

My first thought when I walk through the door of Diamond Lotus Yoga is that Noah has lost his mind.

It's not that I'm bothered by the scents of amber and sandalwood inside, or even by the new-agey chanting music in the background. I don't understand a word of it, but it's kind of relaxing. Still, other than Noah's claim that Amarleen can help me, I don't see why he didn't just have me meet up with her outside of class. I've never been a yoga kind of girl.

I take a deep breath and walk up to the counter. I'm about to ask someone there how to sign up for classes, when I spot a face framed with familiar dark curls. Selena Jensen is standing behind the counter. My ex-best-friend. The girl I never thought I'd see again after her family's going-away party during their last weekend in Boston. I know she moved here, but I didn't think I'd actually run into her. L.A. is supposed to be big.

Selena freezes when she sees me. I'm not sure which is worse—the ice in her hazel eyes now, or the hurt I saw two years ago on the night of the party. I don't have long to think about it, because she quickly turns around and bolts toward the other side of the room. Her hair bobs around her shoulders as she pushes open a door and disappears from view.

"Good morning."

I jump at the greeting and bring my eyes back to the other woman behind the counter.

"Hi. Uh, I'm new here and would like to take a class." I hope I sound convincing, since taking a yoga class is not really on my bucket list of things to do before I go back to The Life-After.

"Well then, let's get you signed up," she says, beaming at me. "You're going to love it."

I wish I could be as optimistic as she is, but something tells me I'm going to end up with a few bruises that might dampen that love just a little bit. If I'm lucky, that's the worst that will happen. Everything I know about yoga tells me I'm going to be trying to bend myself into a pretzel, and even the thought of this hurts.

The woman reaches under the desk and pulls out a sheet of paper and a pen. "I just need you to fill out this form, and then we'll get you all set up."

"Great," I reply, taking the paper and pen from her. I wish I really felt that way.

A few minutes later, I'm rounding a corner and stopping outside of a doorway. There are racks of shoes in the hall. Oh right, yoga is done barefoot. I can't say I'm super thrilled about that. I take my sandals off, though, and then walk into the room.

Dozens of people are already inside, and yoga mats in a rainbow of colors are scattered across the floor. I put my mat down in an empty spot a few feet away from where one girl sits with her eyes closed, her hands resting on her knees.

There's a small stage at the front of the room, raised about two feet off of the ground. It's decorated with fresh flowers, a basket, some framed photos, and a gong. There's nobody on the stage, so it must be where Amarleen sits during class. I try to imagine her. She's probably in her early twenties and toned and flexible beyond belief. I hope she's not one of those teachers who will come and correct my posture while I try to twist my body into a position I'm certain it's not meant for. Not that I've ever taken a yoga class. I'm basing this purely on the fictional yoga teachers I've seen on TV shows and in movies.

I look around me again, and something doesn't fit with my make-believe yoga world. Nobody is dressed in anything spandex. Instead, most people are wearing loose white clothes. Others are in sweatpants and T-shirts or tank tops. Nobody is attempting to show off by perfecting a yoga posture, and only a few people seem concerned about stretching out before class.

A girl sitting across the room catches my eye as I continue to glance around. She smiles at me, and I smile back. Okay, this isn't too hard. Maybe I can pretend to be something other than anti-social for the next hour and a half. Fake it until I make it. That's what I always did when I was Anna.

A woman who looks like she could be in her late forties or early fifties catches my attention as she walks into the room. She's dressed in a flowing white skirt and a loose white shirt, and her hair is wrapped in a white turban. Some of my classmates smile at her and say hello. She returns their smiles while weaving through the maze of mats on the floor. Once she's on the stage, she spreads out a white sheepskin and sits down. This must be Amarleen.

The first thing I notice is that something about her calms me, and it's the kind of calm I felt in The Life-After. The second thing I notice is her energy. Little flecks of gold and silver sparkle everywhere around her. I've only seen those colors surrounding Noah and the people I met in The Life-After. I don't think she's an advisor or a second-timer, though. I mean, wouldn't I know that?

"Sat Nam," Amarleen says, smiling out at us. I have no idea what that means, but everyone in the room repeats it back to her. It's going to be a little hard to fit in around here if these people speak some sort of secret language I don't know. Noah could have warned me about that, at least.

Amarleen asks if there's anyone new in the class today. I think about not raising my hand until I see three other people hold their hands up. I raise mine as far as my shoulder. We're asked to introduce ourselves. Amarleen's eyes linger on me for a few moments after I tell the class my name.

"Thanks for coming today, Cassidy. I feel like—" she pauses, tilting her head to the side and studying me again. "I feel like I need to talk to you about something. Please come see me after class."

I nod, feeling the heat in my cheeks. Noah's going to hear about this one the next time he's brave enough to show himself.

We open the class with our hands pressed together in a position that Amarleen calls prayer pose, chanting a few words I've never heard before. Again with the secret language that everyone but me appears to know. It stops when we start the warm-ups, to my relief. Amarleen tells us that we're working on opening the heart center, which is our fourth chakra. This I understand, at least. I learned all about chakras during my brief time in The Life-After.

I know our class is ninety minutes long, but it seems as though far less time has passed when Amarleen asks us to lie down for a final few minutes of relaxation. Once class is over, I roll up my yoga mat and wait until most of the people have left the room before approaching the stage.

Amarleen pats a space in front of her, inviting me to sit down. I slide onto the stage and sit cross-legged, still not sure why she's called me here.

She closes her eyes and I wonder if I'm supposed to do the same. Before I can, she touches my shoulder and opens her eyes again, looking directly into mine.

"I know what you are," she says, her voice soft.

12

— · —

CHAPTER 12

I'm momentarily dumbstruck. She can't know what I really am.

"What I am?" I repeat.

"You're an angel," she answers, smiling at me. Even her eyes are twinkling.

Not even close. If she only knew.

"I heard that. Give yourself a little more credit." Her smile doesn't waver.

My tongue feels like someone tied it into a double knot. I nod at her, trying to keep my mind blank. It's pretty clear she can read my thoughts just as well as Noah can.

"You've had a life here before," she continues.

I feel my eyes widening and force myself to blink. How does she know this? There's definitely something about her Noah didn't tell me.

She laughs, and I know she's heard what I'm thinking again. "I'm glad you're here. I can tell you're doing some work on clearing a few things out of that old life, and making your energy stronger. That's what brought you here. I think you'll get a lot from this."

It takes a good few seconds to find my voice. "Thank you," I tell her. I'm having trouble thinking of anything else to say.

"I hope I'll keep seeing you here in class," she says.

"I'll be here."

She touches my arm again and I sense our conversation is over. I get up from the stage and take my time collecting my mat and purse. She's still watching me when I walk out of the room.

I don't see Selena at the front desk when I walk by it on my way to the door, and that's probably good. It's painfully clear neither of us knows what to say to the other, and even more obvious she doesn't want to be anywhere near me. Not that I can blame her, really.

I keep walking until I'm outside of Diamond Lotus Yoga and heading down the street to my car. Once I'm sitting inside of it, I dig through my bag to find my phone and turn it on. I sent Riley a text message before coming to class to thank him for dinner last night, but it doesn't look like he's answered me yet. He's probably still sleeping. I would be, too, if Noah hadn't told me to come here.

I put my phone back into my purse and then start the car. After checking the mirrors, I pull out onto the street.

"So what did you think?" a voice asks from beside me.

I slam on the brakes. "Geez, don't do that while I'm driving!"

Noah chuckles from where he sits in the passenger seat. "It's an empty street. The worst thing that can happen is you'll drive over a leaf."

"It's still dangerous," I grumble, releasing the brake and moving my foot back to the gas pedal.

"Did you enjoy meeting Amarleen?"

I nod, but say nothing.

"You want to ask me something, don't you?" he says.

Of course he knows what's on my mind. It would sure be nice if I could turn the tables and read his mind for a day.

"How does she do that?" I ask.

"Do what?"

"What you do." I bring the car to a stop at a red light. "Is she supposed to be able to do that?"

"You mean read your thoughts?"

"Yeah, that. It's something someone in The Life-After would do, but she's here and even I can't do that here."

"Amarleen's energy is at a very high level. It's higher than yours."

Well, obviously. But that still doesn't answer my question.

"If it's that high, shouldn't she be in The Life-After?" The light turns green and I start driving again.

"She could be in The Life-After if she wanted to be," he says. "She almost was."

"She didn't go, though?" The thought of refusing The Life-After seems impossible. I'll always remember the moment I first opened my eyes there, with the warmth radiating through me and the colors and lights everywhere. You don't just say no to that.

"She wanted to stay to finish a job she knew was her calling."

"What? Teaching yoga?" Right. He has to be making this up.

"You see it like that, but that's not what she's doing."

"So enlighten me. I just finished meditating, I'm sure that makes it easier."

Uh oh. He's giving me a warning look now. Maybe he's actually serious.

"Amarleen helps others raise their energy," he says. "Some of her students will go on to do the same thing she's doing right now. She's not a second-timer, but she's helped a lot of people through their darkest times in the same way second-timers do."

"She knows so much, though," I persist. "What happens if she tells someone about The Life-After and what life here really is?"

He shakes his head. "Her energy is highly—and I mean highly—evolved. She can see how telling people about The Life-After could harm them more than it could help them."

I slow the car down as I approach an intersection. "Does she know you?" I ask, putting on the car's turn signal.

He nods. "She does. Because her energy is ready for The Life-After, she's able to see advisors visiting The Before just like you can. She came up to me one day when I was with another second-timer and told me she knew what I was. We had coffee, and I started dropping in on her classes."

Of course she can see Noah and any other advisor who might be around. She probably connects to The Life-After just like I do, too.

"She does," Noah answers. "She connects when she meditates."

He starts to say something else, but my phone interrupts him. The ringtone tells me it's either my aunt or my uncle, so I let it ring.

"You should get that," Noah says. I have no doubt he knows I'm trying to dodge my aunt and uncle right now.

"I can't. It's illegal to talk on my phone and drive." This is true, actually. It's a California law.

"Not hands-free." He points at the microphone clipped to the sun visor.

I have no idea how he knows this stuff, given he hasn't lived in The Before since well before cell phones and laws about them were invented. The guy died before phones even had keypads.

"It can wait," I mumble. Then I hear my uncle's voice coming from the phone speaker.

"Cassidy?"

I can't believe Noah pressed the answer button. I'd give him a dirty look, but now I have to try and focus on watching the road and talking to my uncle without either becoming a major disaster.

"Cassidy?" my uncle repeats.

"Hey, Uncle Mike," I say. "Sorry, bad connection. Maybe I should call you back later."

"It sounds fine on this end. Keep talking, and we'll see if it drops."

I come to a stop at a red light and look over at the passenger seat. It's empty. Of course Noah abandoned ship at the first opportunity and left me to deal with this on my own. Some advisor he is.

I let go of the breath I'm holding. "Okay. What's up?"

"Did you get my message from the other night?" my uncle asks.

The light turns green. I press down on the gas pedal. "I've been a little busy this week. Remind me?"

"The letter that came from Harvard about you declining their offer."

"Right. I'll call them tomorrow." Or never. My uncle doesn't have to know that. With any luck, nothing else will show up in the mail before I go back to The Life-After. He and my aunt will probably forget all about it once I'm gone.

"You don't need to. Your aunt already called them."

A squirrel darts in front of the car. I slam on my brakes.

"Sh-sh-she did?" I stutter. I wasn't counting on that.

"She did. It looks like the mistake wasn't on their end."

I open my mouth to speak, but words seem to be failing me. I close my mouth again, watching the squirrel cross safely to the sidewalk.

"Why didn't you tell us about this?" Yup. He's mad.

"I was going to," I lie, trying to come up with a believable excuse for why I'd cancel on Harvard. I use the first one I can think of. "I think I just need a year off. Like a gap year."

"Just so you know, your aunt is going to co—"

I interrupt him. "Hey, Uncle Mike, you're starting to break up. I'll call you later and we can finish talking about this on a land line." I press the button to end the call before he can answer me.

If I'm lucky, I'll figure out how to deal with this before my uncle or aunt talks to me again. It's exactly what I don't need to be worrying about right now.

13

CHAPTER 13

When five days pass with no word from Riley, I'm pretty sure something is up with him, or maybe with his phone. The text messages I sent all went through, though, and are even marked as read. His voicemail picked up the one time I tried calling. This leaves me with one conclusion: it's him. Okay, it's what he thinks about me. If I had to guess, I'd say my birthday dinner was a date and I blew it big time. That's exactly what I'd want to happen under normal circumstances, but this is about as far from normal as anything gets. It's his fault for not making it a pity dinner.

Now I'm left with a huge problem. If Riley is avoiding me, then I can't help him. If I can't help him, then both of us are in big trouble. And it's not like I can show up at his doorstep and insist we hang out. For one thing, that's pretty much like stalking him. For another, I don't even know where he lives.

Any brilliant advice, Noah? I think. The only sound I hear is clothes dropping onto the floor as I rummage through one of my still-unpacked suitcases, looking for my running shoes. Yeah, I should have known.

I toss a shirt out of the suitcase. There's one shoe, anyway. I start to reach for it but stop when the doorbell rings.

That's weird. No one in L.A. but Riley knows where I live, so it's either him ringing my doorbell, or it's some door-to-door solicitor. I'm pretty sure solicitors don't canvass houses in the Hollywood Hills, though. With so many of the houses behind locked gates, I can't see how it would be worth their time. I leave the running shoe where it is and get up to see who's at the front door.

The doorbell rings seven more times in the few seconds it takes me to get there. "All right, already," I say out loud, rounding the corner into the foyer. Then I stop mid-step.

My aunt is standing on my doorstep, and I can see her scowling face through the pane of glass beside the door. It's too late to run back to my bedroom and pretend nobody's home, mainly because she's peering through the window and staring straight at me. She looks far from happy. I'd rather walk barefoot on burning coals than deal with an unhappy Aunt Sarah, but I've already been spotted.

I curse under my breath and square my shoulders. Then I take another two steps and reach for the door handle, knowing full well I'm letting a human hurricane into my house.

"Took you long enough," she snaps when I open the door. As usual, not a single auburn hair on her head is out of place. I can't spot even the slightest wrinkle in the fabric of her tailored pantsuit. Her blue eyes are icy cold, which is no different from the last time I looked into them before I left Boston. It's possible they're icier than Selena's were when I saw her at the yoga studio, and that's hard to beat.

My aunt pushes past me, stepping inside the house. It's then I see her two large suitcases on the doorstep. That's definitely not a good sign. The last thing I need is my aunt setting up camp in my house.

"Wh—what are you doing here?" I ask, looking at her and then back to the suitcases. I think I saw a horror movie start this way once.

"I flew out this morning," she says, waving her hand to dismiss my question as though flying across the country and showing up unannounced at my house in L.A. is the most normal thing in the world. "Could you make yourself useful and get my suitcases before you shut the door?"

I hear her. I don't make a move for her suitcases, though, or shut the door.

"Why are you here? Aren't you missing your ladies' lunch or something?" She never misses that lunch. It's how she catches up on the neighborhood gossip.

"I'm here to take you home," she says, sounding surprised. "What did you think was going to happen after you pulled that stunt with Harvard?" She gives a little huff when she realizes I'm not moving, and walks past me again to retrieve her suitcases from outside.

Of course. This is my punishment. Reminding her I'm now eighteen years old and legally out from under her thumb is likely to have the same effect as yelling in a wind tunnel.

"I am home," I remind her, although I'm sure these are all wasted words. "This is my house, if you've forgotten. It officially became mine on my birthday."

She rolls one of her suitcases into the foyer. "No, dear. You're going home to Boston, where you're starting college in a few weeks. You're not staying out here."

"The hell I'm not."

"Watch your language, young lady." The second suitcase rolls past me and she stops, letting go of the handle and putting her hands on her hips. "No niece of mine is going to waste her life as a college dropout, boozing and partying it up in Hollywood. I'm not letting you rot your brain until you're just some junkie, squandering the money your parents left you."

I stare at her. "What movie did you get that from? I don't drink, I don't party, and I'm sure not a junkie. And by the way, you can't drop out of college if you haven't even started yet." Yeah, that last point probably won't fly. It's true, though.

"Oh, you're starting. I'm not about to let you wreck your future just because you feel like it."

The woman is hopeless. I count backwards from ten before answering her.

"I'm not going with you, so you can turn around now and go right back to Boston. I'll call Uncle Mike and tell him when your flight gets in."

A tight smile appears on my aunt's face. "It's a nice thought, but you have to come with me. I've already spoken to the dean of admissions and assured him it was all a misunderstanding. That took a lot of work, but I got you back in for the fall semester. I suggest you wipe that look off your face and go pack your bags."

Same Aunt Sarah. It always has to be her way. Not this time, though. I can't go anywhere until my job is done, and the only place I'm going then is The Life-After.

"I'm not going back to Boston," I repeat. "And I'm not talking about this anymore."

"Fine," she says, walking past me and down the hall into the living room. I follow her. Sudden acceptance without a full-blown tantrum definitely doesn't sound like my aunt when she isn't getting her way.

"Fine?" I echo.

"Mmm-hmm." She sits down on the sofa.

"So you're going home, then?" I ask.

"No," she answers, a smile still fixed on her face. "This just shows me you can't be trusted to make decisions for yourself. Eighteen or not, you clearly still need adult supervision, so I think I'll stay for a while. It's for your own good."

No, this isn't a horror movie. This is the very definition of hell.

14

CHAPTER 14

"I need a nap," I mumble, turning away from my aunt and heading back to the hallway.

"Don't worry, I'll still be here when you get up," she calls after me. "Maybe we can work on your hosting manners then."

Wonderful. It's hard enough trying to help Riley when he's stopped answering his phone and I have no idea how to find him and no clue what it is I'm supposed to do if I somehow manage to see him again. Now I have to deal with an overbearing chaperone who makes Noah look like a pushover with the personality of pure sunshine.

I fling myself face-first onto my bed once I get to my bedroom, burying my head in the pillows. I stay there, not moving, until I doze off.

When I wake up an hour later, the strains of classical music coming from the living room remind me that my aunt's arrival wasn't just a bad dream. Spotting the running shoe I left in my suitcase earlier, I carefully get up from my bed, trying not to make a sound. After digging through the rest of the clothes in the suitcase, I locate the matching shoe. With a shoe in each hand, I tiptoe down the hall in the opposite direction from the living room. I put on my shoes once I'm safely out on the veranda, looking up every few seconds to make sure my aunt isn't watching me from one of the windows. I need to get out of here for a while.

It's already half past seven when I jog through the gates of Runyon Canyon Park. Weaving in and out of the families and couples walking down to the base of the canyon, I concentrate on the crunch of the dirt trail beneath my feet. It doesn't matter that it's warm enough outside for sweat to drip from my hairline in seconds, or that almost everyone else here is smart enough to be walking instead of running on the trail. If I can focus on putting one foot in front of the other and just breathing, then I can put the last few days out of my mind. Forget about how I'm going to help Riley, and forget about my aunt. Just jog, and just breathe.

I round a curve in the trail, and a pile of flowers and unlit candles sitting at the bottom of a nearby slope catches my eye. A middle-aged woman kneels in front of it, and I watch her place a card beside a candle in a glass jar. I can see tears on her cheeks when she stands up. The energy around her and around the candles, flowers, and her card tells me this is a memorial site for somebody.

I know people mourn and grieve what they see as loss of life not only because of someone's physical absence, but also because they have no way of knowing what comes next, or if there's anything at all. They don't know grief happens mostly because they can no longer feel the energy of someone who's passed away. When two people are very close, whether they're family, friends, or two people in love, their energy connects. When someone can't feel the energy of their loved one anymore they feel loss, but think it's because they'll never see that person again. They don't know how much the energy connection has to do with it, and don't understand it until they get to The Life-After and are aware of the other person's energy again.

I wish I could tell the grieving woman what I know and make her believe that none of this life here is what she thinks it is. I can't, though. That's the hardest part of being a second-timer. So I do what little I can, jogging past her and connecting my energy to hers in the hopes it will boost her a bit and help her feel a moment or two of peace. I bring my energy back closer to me when she disappears from view.

I stop for a drink of water when I reach the canyon's first plateau. The view of the city from here is spectacular. I remember a long ago summer afternoon when I sat at the end of the plateau with David, the rush of my legs dangling off the edge mixing with the high of watching the sunset with the person I loved. There's a tree here somewhere that David carved our initials in, D.B. + A.M. If it's still here, it's the only marker left of our time together. There are a lot of trees here, though, and it's been a long time.

"Nice view," a voice says. I turn my head to see some guy who looks like he's in his forties leering at me. Yeah, this is almost what I need tonight.

All I can do is ignore him, so I shrug and take a step in the other direction. I keep walking until I reach a steep incline with built-in stairs made of railway ties leading up to the next plateau. As I do, I bump into someone else. This someone is much younger than the guy behind me, and he looks uncomfortable. That's probably because he's been ignoring my text messages since he left me standing in my driveway on my birthday.

"Hi." The one word is all I can think to say to Riley. If this was anyone else, I'd probably just keep going. There's no rule about ignoring the person you're supposed to be helping, but I'm pretty sure it's not a great idea.

"Hey." Riley wipes his forehead with the back of his hand, shifting his eyes away from me. He shuffles from one foot to the other, and I wonder if he knows he's doing it. Probably not.

"Out for a run?" I ask. Like that's not obvious or anything.

"Just clearing my head. I come here to do that." He kicks at a pebble on the ground. I watch it fall down the side of the canyon.

"It's a good place for it." The leering guy walks past us, shooting Riley a disgusted look. I ignore him. "So, I, uh—" I stop for a moment, wondering when I got so bad at this. When I was Anna, I would have known exactly what to say or I would have improvised something on the spot. That's just how I was, then. I take a deep breath, trying to channel anything of her that might still be left in me, and try again. "I sent you a couple of texts after my birthday. Did you get them?"

I watch his energy carefully. There's definitely some guilt there, and I can see him draw his energy closer around him like full-body armor. Not so fast.

I expand my energy out to meet his, but his energy is being stubborn tonight. It takes some effort to force my energy through, but I keep going until I feel the tingle and pull of our energy connecting.

I watch Riley relax as our energy meets. The set of his jaw softens.

"Yeah, I did," he says, blinking a few times. "I meant to answer those, and I'm glad I ran into you. We should do something again soon."

Energy is a funny thing, sometimes. A minute ago, I know he would have bolted if given the chance. Now that we're connected, though, and he isn't able to put up a shield, I think he means what he says and the words seem to be coming from a different place. Fear is what makes someone put up an energy shield, I know. I just can't put my finger on what he could possibly be afraid of.

"We should," I agree. I take a step toward the stairs, knowing he'll follow from the pull of my energy on his.

"Have you ever been here before?" he asks, walking beside me.

"No, but I've been meaning to come here since I got to L.A. I've just been busy getting settled in, and it's been so warm." It's not really a lie, since I haven't been here in this particular body.

"It's amazing, right?" He takes a step up and steadies himself, then reaches his arm out to me. I grab hold of his hand and let him help me up to where he is. His fingers send electrical currents through mine.

"Amazing," I say. We're high enough now to see pools in the backyards of mansions below us. "Do you come here a lot?"

"Every week. On a clear day like today, you can see even see way out to where I live."

"Where's that?"

"Santa Monica." He points out toward the coastline. I can just barely make out where the ocean meets the shore. "Have you been out there yet?"

"No, but I'd like to see it soon." In truth, I spent a lot of time in Santa Monica when I was Anna. I just haven't seen it since.

"It's great. You should come and see it sometime."

"I'd like to do that," I tell him. The tingling is stronger now, and I know that's a good sign.

We keep climbing up the path until we reach the next plateau. Riley takes a drink of water from his water bottle while I stand for a moment, trying to catch a breeze from any direction. The air is still, though. Looking out over the city, I watch the last glimmer of sunlight twinkling above the ocean.

I raise my sunglasses off of my eyes and let them perch on top of my head. Riley comes to stand beside me and we say nothing, watching the painted streaks of daylight fade to twilight.

When we turn around to head to the road that leads back to the bottom of the canyon, I spot the tree David carved our initials in. Even from far away I can see the letters on the trunk, but that's not what makes me stop walking. There's a white feather below the tree, so large and bright it almost lights itself up against the growing darkness.

"Is something wrong?" Riley asks, trying to follow my line of sight to see what I'm looking at. His eyes pass right over the feather.

I shake my head. "No, I'm just a little more out of breath than I thought. I guess I should hike more."

We walk past the tree and I leave the feather where it is. I let Riley do most of the talking as we make our way down the winding road to the bottom of the canyon.

CHAPTER 15

C ountdown to The Life-After: five weeks.

"Where are you going?" my aunt yells from the kitchen. So much for trying to sneak out.

"To see a friend. Please feel free to go back to Boston while I'm out." I don't know if she can hear me, and I don't care either way.

The house has been a war zone for the last few days, and these are the first words we've spoken to one another in over twenty-four hours. The silence started after an airport limo showed up in the driveway yesterday morning, the driver claiming to have instructions to take me to LAX. Even the pleading phone call I made to my uncle to talk some sense into Aunt Sarah fell on deaf ears, but I guess I shouldn't have expected anything different. We're a Harvard family, after all—that's where my uncle and aunt met. No one in our family tree dares to put college off for a year, and the only one to defy the Harvard tradition was my mother. She went to Stanford, which made her the black sheep of the family. Ivory towers can be a little strange.

My aunt appears in the foyer just as I'm turning the handle of the front door.

"Who is this friend?" she demands. "Not some boy you haven't introduced me to, I hope." Here we go.

"A vagrant who lives out on Skid Row," I answer.

"It is a boy, isn't it?" she narrows her eyes. "That's what's behind this dropping-out-of-Harvard nonsense."

I ignore her, pulling open the door. She presses her hand against it, trying to push it shut. I yank harder, forcing her to move her hand away. I win.

"Have a good day," I mumble, stepping out onto the front porch.

"A little respect would be nice, you know," she calls after me. Yeah, ditto.

I pretend I don't hear her and keep walking to my car. She's still standing there when I back down the driveway, and I can tell she's furious. I give her a wave before zooming away down the street.

It takes about half an hour to drive to Santa Monica. I follow the instructions of my GPS turn-for-turn, but I'm sure it must be wrong when I pull up outside of the address Riley gave me for his apartment. Either that, or he gave me the address for his parents' recording studio by mistake. It sure looks like a studio, complete with two skinny guys with black spiky hair standing outside. Both of them are wearing black T-shirts and jeans. They could definitely be musicians working on a record. This can't be Riley's place.

I park my car anyway, then pull out my phone to call him. Before I can open my contacts list, though, a knock on my car window makes me jump. I look up to see Riley standing outside.

"You live in a recording studio?" I ask, opening the door and getting out of the car.

He laughs. "Kind of. I live above it. My parents own the whole building. They let me move in when I started college last fall."

"Doesn't it get loud?"

"Only when there's a metal band recording." He leads me to a set of stairs around the side of the building. I follow him up the steps to a door at the top.

"It must take you forever to get to work," I tease him.

"The stairs take at least five seconds."

He opens the door, letting me walk ahead of him. The inside of his apartment is bright, with the sunlight from the windows reflecting off white walls. There's wall-to-wall carpet in the living room, probably to deaden some of the sound from the studio below. If there's anyone recording right now, I can't hear them up here.

"Soundproofing," he comments, as if reading my mind. "See? It's really not so bad. Want something to drink?"

I follow him over to the kitchen. "I could do with a glass of Dom Perignon."

"You're in luck. I have water, and I think I saw some juice in there last week."

"Water it is," I tell him.

He opens the fridge and takes out a pitcher, then pours each of us a glass.

"Cheers," he says, raising his glass to me. He drains it in two gulps, then sets his glass down on the counter.

I take my time looking around, pausing when I spot a Nintendo Switch controller on the living room coffee table.

"A Switch guy, are you? What game?"

"Mario Kart."

"Kid stuff," I scoff.

"That sounds like a challenge."

"Game on," I tell him, putting my glass on the counter. He raises an eyebrow at me and walks out of the kitchen, into the living room.

"Prepare to eat your words."

I follow behind him. "Nah, I'll just watch you choke on my dust."

He sits down on the sofa. I see the determined glint in his eyes. "Those are fighting words, girl. Don't say I didn't warn you."

He starts the game and it's not long before it becomes a mad war of driving. In the first round, I drive him right off the road and cross the finish line before he can get back on the racetrack. In the second round, it's his turn to smoke me. His arms shoot up in victory and I can't help but chuckle at the little-boy look on his face.

He slings an arm around my shoulder. "Ready to re-live that?" He turns his head to face me, glee in his eyes.

"We're tied, buddy."

"For the next three minutes, maybe. You're going down."

"Shut up and hit play."

He grins at me, but makes no move for the controller. It's then I notice how close his face is to mine. He's only inches away. If I'm not crazy, he's getting closer, only I can't tell if he's moving closer to me or if I'm moving closer to him. The tingling is back, too, sweeping over me from head to toe.

"Ry?" a female voice calls out. There's a quick knock, then the sound of a door being opened. I move my face away from Riley's and look over his shoulder to see a woman walk inside his apartment.

"Dr. Julian's office called. Your ti—" she stops when her eyes land on me. "Oh, I'm sorry. I didn't realize you had company."

I expect a suspicious look from her, since I'm some girl she doesn't know and I'm up here alone with her son. It doesn't happen. If anything, her face lights up.

"Hey, Mom." Riley shoots up off of the sofa. His face is flushed.

I stand up, too. Riley doesn't move, but I walk over to his mom and extend my hand.

"Nice to meet you. I'm Cassidy."

"Elizabeth," she says, taking my hand. It's easy to see that Riley has her eyes. While his look a little nervous, I see a question in hers. She's probably trying to figure out if we're friends, or if there's something more going on.

"We were just playing Mario Kart," I say, the words rushing out of my mouth. I don't know why I feel like I need to explain that. Our game controllers were right in front of us, and it's not like she caught us doing something. Maybe it's because Riley's face is now positively crimson.

"I didn't mean to interrupt you guys," she says, and looks past me to her son. "Ry, I just came to tell you that you have a new time with Dr. Julian this week."

You don't have to be able to read energy to notice something weird going on here. Riley's mom is leaning against the doorframe, now looking at both of us, and she probably doesn't even realize she has the biggest smile growing on her face. Riley's looking at the floor.

"The band scheduled to come in tonight just canceled, too," she adds. "That means the studio is free after seven if you and John want to use it."

"Thanks. I'll see what he's up to." Riley sits back down on the sofa, his face still a little pink. Interesting.

"All right. I'll let you two get back to your game." She nods at the game controllers. "Nice to meet you, Cassidy."

"Nice to meet you, too," I say.

She smiles at me again and then walks out of the apartment, closing the door behind her. Riley stares at the carpet, even after the door clicks shut. I walk back over to the sofa and sit down beside him.

"Doctor's appointment?" I ask.

"Something like that," he answers, turning back to the TV. Our game is still paused.

"Your mom seems cool," I tell him.

"Yeah." That's all he says. I watch him take out his phone and type something. He's probably sending a text about studio time to the friend his mom mentioned. I'd give anything right now for the ability to read his thoughts, or for Noah to come help me out. I search my mind for something else to say.

"What are you working on in the studio?" I lean forward to grab my controller from where I set it down on the coffee table, hoping he'll do the same thing. He doesn't.

"Just a side project with one of my buddies."

"Are you playing guitar on it?" I ask, looking at a guitar stand beside the TV. There's an acoustic guitar held up in it, and the worn spots on the body tell me it's been played quite a bit.

"Guitar and vocals." He puts his phone down.

We're definitely not picking up where we left off. I look around the room for something I can talk about to fill the silence. The first thing I see that looks conversation-worthy is a framed photograph on the table beside the sofa. In it, a younger-looking Riley stands beside a girl with cascades of strawberry blond hair. Both of them grin at the camera.

"Is that one of your sisters?" I ask.

He turns his head to see what I'm looking at. When his eyes land on the photo, his lips press together in a thin line.

"No, just someone I was close to." His voice is quiet.

"Is this from when you were in high school?"

"Yup."

"Are you still close?" The words are out of my mouth before I realize the question makes me sound like a prying girlfriend. I try to think of something to say that will let him know that's not how I meant it. I come up with nothing.

"She died."

That's not the answer I expected. A shiver runs through me, but not from his words. It takes me a minute to realize it's because his energy is retreating, drawing in around him again, just like it did on my birthday. He went silent for a few days after that, which can't happen again. We don't have time. I need to keep him talking.

"Do you miss her?" I ask.

"Yup."

Well, that question didn't do much. He gets up from the sofa and takes the guitar out of the stand. I can see grief rising in his energy, as tightly closed around him as it is.

"She's still with you, you know." I watch him sit down in a chair that's a few feet away and raise the guitar up on one knee. I wish I could tell him there's no reason to grieve.

"I don't talk about her."

The tone of his voice warns me not to push this any further, but something tells me to keep going. Maybe what I find out about him and this girl could help me unlock the great mystery of why I'm here, assigned to him.

16

CHAPTER 16

"**M**aybe you should talk about her."

Riley shrugs and strums a few chords on the guitar.

"Did you love her?" I ask.

He keeps strumming. A minute passes, notes filling the air, and then the music stops. He puts down the guitar pick.

"I knew her for most of my life. So yes, I loved her." He leans the guitar against the side of the chair and then stands up.

I watch him head for the kitchen. I should really quit while I'm ahead, but again, something tells me not to stop.

"Did she know?"

He opens the fridge door. I get up from the sofa and move to a counter stool that's closer to him. He stops rummaging through the fridge and shuts the door again, his hands empty.

"What kind of—" he starts to say, then stops and takes a breath, raking a hand through his hair. "There's a lot I never got to tell her. It doesn't matter now."

"Why do you think it doesn't matter?"

"Why do you think it does?" His eyes are on me now.

"Just because she's gone in body, doesn't mean you can't talk to her."

"Yeah, talking to thin air is exactly what sane people do."

"She's not thin air." He raises an eyebrow at me. "Have you tried talking to her?" I ask.

I watch his lips part like he's about to say something, then he closes his mouth again. A quick check of his energy shows me sparks that are the colors of confusion, grief, and even a bit of anger.

"Enough, okay?" he says after a moment.

"She just seems like she was important to you." I keep my voice quiet and calm, hoping it will soothe his energy. "Saying what you need to say might help, even if you think you're talking to nothing more than air."

I wait for silence. He surprises me, though.

"It sounds like you've thought about this quite a bit." He studies me, looking thoughtful. "Maybe a little too much for an eighteen-year-old."

If he only knew. His energy is settling a bit, so that's good at least. I close my eyes for a moment and try to come up with an answer for him.

"I talk to my parents a lot. It helps me." It sounds plausible, or I think it does.

He pauses. I watch his chest rise as he takes a deep breath, then fall again as he lets it out.

"I forgot," he finally says. "I'm sorry."

"Don't be." I smile at him. "It's a normal part of my life, and talking to them makes me happy. I thought maybe it could help you, too."

"Help me how?"

"Let go of the grief." I sense he's about to argue, but he stops himself. The crease across his forehead tells me he's considering what I'm saying. Maybe it even makes sense to him.

The crease vanishes as he seems to come to a decision. "Yeah, well." He shrugs, looking out the window. "This is life, not a dress rehearsal. There's nothing after this."

"What if there is, though?" I insist. What if I know there is, and that this life you think is life is actually nothing compared to what comes next?

"Then what would be the point of this?"

I want to tell him that all of this is about getting ready for the next phase, and that he wouldn't think this way if he could see the things I have. I can't tell him this, though, or at least not in those words. But there are other ways I can put it.

"Maybe this is like being a caterpillar before becoming the butterfly," I say.

"Why wouldn't we know, then?" he argues.

"We only know what we can see. If we're like the caterpillar in the cocoon, we can only see the shell around us until we break out and fly free." So I sound like some cheesy short story from a high school English class. It's not my fault The Life-After won't let me say what I want to.

He puts his hands on the counter, leaning against it. He doesn't look happy. "I get that's what you believe, and it's fine if it helps you get through the day. Just don't push it on me, okay?"

"Okay."

I don't know if he hears me. Something about his energy tells me that for the moment, he's far away from here, reliving a memory I could see if I were Noah. I can guess it involves the girl in the photograph.

I excuse myself to find the bathroom, although I don't have to use it. I'm just not sure what else to do. I stay locked inside the small room for a minute or two longer than I need to after washing my hands.

When I hear notes from the guitar, I know it's safe to go back out. Riley's in the living room now, sitting on the chair and holding the guitar again.

"Serenading me, are you?" I make sure there's a teasing edge in my voice so my words come across as joking, and not flirting. I see a smirk cross his lips.

"Definitely." He hits the first few chords of something that distinctly belongs to the heavy metal and hair-band days of my time as Anna. It's so thrashing and choppy, I'm surprised I don't see pieces of the guitar pick flying through the air.

"Better than the banjos, I guess."

"I swear we've got to do something about your music appreciation." He puts the guitar down beside the chair.

"I appreciate music just fine." I lean over and pick up the guitar, then take it to the sofa where I sit and pluck each of the strings to see if it's in tune. It's not. I turn the keys at the top of the neck, plucking each string until the notes that fill my ears sound like they should. I'm aware Riley is watching me. I keep my eyes on the guitar.

"You play."

"Can I see that pick you were destroying?" I ask.

The thin piece of plastic lands beside me on the sofa. Taking it between my fingers, I bring it to the strings, wrapping the fingers of my other hand around the instrument's neck. I gaze at the floor and begin strumming a song I wrote last summer in my bedroom at my aunt and uncle's house. When I get to the end of it, I let the notes fade away into the room and open my eyes again.

"Don't stop."

I turn my head to look at Riley. He looks curious, and maybe a little awe-struck.

"How long have you been playing?" he asks.

"Since I was a kid." I stop short of telling him my dad had a guitar that became mine when he left this life, and that I picked it up as soon as my aunt and uncle would let me. It doesn't seem like a good time to be talking about people who've moved on to The Life-After.

"Does it have lyrics?" he asks.

"Just melody," I say. "You don't want to hear me sing." I couldn't carry a tune if my life depended on it, so I've never seen the point in writing lyrics for my songs. I'm lucky enough to have gotten away with learning to play the guitar.

My aunt wasn't thrilled when the guitar first made an appearance, but she had enough tact to not take my father's instrument away from me. The trade-off was being forced into piano lessons, too, but at least she stopped there. I could have ended up in ballet classes three times a week, another pirouetting bunhead like the daughters of my aunt's friends.

"You're going to play me more," he says, sounding very matter-of-fact.

"Is that a request or a warning?" I ask, getting up from the sofa to put the guitar back in its stand.

"It might be both."

"I'll think about it."

He picks up a game controller from the table. "If I win the next round of Mario Kart, you're playing more."

"Game on, my friend. Game on." I sit down and pick up the other controller.

We spend the afternoon playing video games and taking turns playing his guitar. He stays on the chair across from the sofa instead of moving to sit beside me, so there's no repeat of the moment that happened before his mom came to the door. If that even was a moment. I leave a little while before his friend John is supposed to show up for some studio time.

"'Til the next time you beg for Mario Kart mercy," I tell him, as he walks me down the stairs and around the corner to my car.

"It was an off afternoon. Show me some sympathy." He stretches his arms out for a hug.

"You had home TV advantage," I counter, letting him wrap his arms around me. He hugs me for longer than he usually does. I should pull away, but the tingling starts and I know it's a good sign. We're connecting again.

"Riley!" The shout from behind us makes me jump, and then there's a good few inches between Riley and me again. He blinks hard, then raises his hand and waves at someone.

I turn around to see who he's waving at and almost lose my balance. This can't be for real.

Selena stands at the end of the driveway leading up to a house across the street. Our eyes meet for less than a second, but it's long enough for a dark look to wash over her face. It vanishes almost instantly when her eyes shift back to Riley.

"My dad wants to know if you and Bill are coming over to watch the game tomorrow," she calls out, bringing her hand up above her eyes to shield them from the sun.

"I think so," he calls back, and then looks down at me. "Bill is my dad."

I bite the inside of my lip. Riley knows Selena. In fact, it looks like she's his neighbor. And now Selena knows that I know Riley. Something tells me this probably isn't good.

I smile and push my sunglasses down over my eyes. "Have fun in the studio tonight, and I guess watching the game tomorrow."

"We'll talk soon," he says. I feel Selena's eyes on us and I know it's time to get out of here.

Riley stays standing by the curb while I unlock my car door and get inside, and he doesn't move when I give him a wave and pull out onto the road. I can still see him there when I get to the stop sign at the end of the street, a speck in the distance watching after me. Selena's there, too, standing in her driveway, her arms folded across her chest.

17

CHAPTER 17

I might be breaking a world record for yawning. It's probably not a great record to break while driving on the freeway, but I can't help it, no matter how hard I try. My energy level is low after my visit with Riley, although not to the point of blacking out. That hasn't happened since the night of my birthday, but I feel weak enough to know that I need to be in Amarleen's class in the morning.

It's a relief to pull into my driveway, even though I know I'll be walking into a snake pit. I'm not too sure I'm up for round five-hundred-and-three with my aunt, but there's a nap waiting for me once I get past her. That's all the motivation I need to open my door and get out of the car.

I square my shoulders like I'm getting ready for battle. Which I am, really. Breathe in, breathe out, and just keep walking.

My aunt flings open the front door before I can put my key in the lock. "You're late," she barks.

"For what?" I brush past her. I'm only a few steps away from my bed and the beauty of burying myself under the blankets. Give me strength.

"Dinner. You know we always eat at six o'clock. Sharp."

I kick off my sandals, not bothering to turn around to look at her. "That's when you eat at your house."

"And that's when we'll eat here, since you're grounded. You're not just running off to see God-knows-what-boy and not telling me when you're coming home."

I shrug and keep walking, dragging my feet down the hallway to my bedroom. "You can't ground me," I call over my shoulder. "We're not at your house, remember?"

I shut and lock my bedroom door behind me before she can answer, and then sink face-first into my bed. All I want to do is curl up under the covers and get swept away into dreamland, but I know what I have to do before I let myself sleep.

It takes a few minutes before I can push myself up with my arms. Once I'm up, I close my eyes and let my mind go still. It takes longer than usual before I see the sparks of gold that tell me I'm connecting.

I must nod off while I'm getting my energy boost, because it's after 1 a.m. when my eyes open and I look at the clock on my bedside table. My head fell forward at some point, and my neck is stiff from the position I've been sleeping in. Fantastic. I try rubbing it with my fingers.

As sleepy as I was before, I'm wide-awake now. The house is silent, and I know my aunt went to bed hours ago. The quiet gives me a chance to think, but I'm not sure that's a good thing. Between my aunt's house-crashing and life-crashing, running into Selena again and finding out she knows Riley, and then Riley himself, there's a lot to think about.

There's something nagging at my mind, too. I sit still, trying to let the thought surface. The moment Riley's mom walked into his apartment plays in my head, almost on a loop, until I realize what it is.

Dr. Julian's office called, and there was something about a new time to see him. Elizabeth didn't say what the appointment was for and neither did Riley, but I think I need to find out.

I grab my iPad from my bedside table and open a web browser. Dr. Julian and Los Angeles are what I type in the search box, even though there are probably a zillion or so doctors in L.A. with the same last name.

Or maybe not. I stare at the first search result that shows up on my screen. Ernest Julian, Ph.D. Grief counselor.

Is Riley seeing a grief counselor? I think of the photograph in his living room and what happened to his energy when he was talking about the girl pictured in it. Then there's how uncomfortable he is with any mention of death at all. This might even make sense.

"Did you have a nice date this afternoon?"

I look up from the screen at the sound of Noah's voice. Now I know I'm onto something. Noah doesn't usually show up in the middle of the night without sending me an indigo feather first.

I ignore his question. "Riley's seeing a grief counselor?" I ask. He nods. "Because of the girl in the photograph?"

"Good detective skills." That must be a yes.

"Who was she?"

"Her name was Amanda." I wait for more, but there's nothing. Helpful, Noah.

"Am I here to help him with his grief over Amanda?" I ask.

"Yes."

"I don't get it, though. He's already seeing a grief counselor. Why does he need me?"

Noah sets his hat down beside him on the chair. "Let me show you something."

"Can you do that here?" It's been a long time since he's shown me anything. The last time he did was shortly after I found myself in The Life-After, and I thought maybe he could only do it there.

He smiles. "Close your eyes and clear your mind, just like you do when you connect to The Life-After."

My mind is a complete blank for what feels like a minute or two, and then a blur of colors appear. As the blur comes into focus, I see motion in front of me.

I think I'm watching something that happened here in L.A. but can't be sure at first. The strawberry-blond girl from the photograph is in front of me, standing outside of a brick building. The sign on the building tells me it's a high school. This is Amanda. She looks like she's waiting for someone, bouncing from foot to foot. When she spots something and smiles, I follow her gaze and see a younger-looking Riley come walking toward her.

Something pulls my eyes down to their hands, which are only a few inches apart as they walk side by side. It takes a few moments for me to realize what I'm supposed to be looking at isn't their hands or their faces at all, but their energy. More specifically, her energy. I focus in on the waves of light around her. My eyes almost fly open at what I see, but Noah places a hand on my shoulder to help me stay focused on what I need to be watching.

I can tell from Amanda's energy that she's a second-timer, or at least she was. This must be a glimpse of her time in The Before prior to her return to The Life-After, but I'm not sure I understand why she was with Riley. I'm the one assigned to him. How Amanda fits in is a mystery.

The pressure from Noah's fingers on my shoulder gets a little heavier. I stop thinking about Amanda and why she's here, and focus on her energy to read it for more clues. Her energy plays with Riley's and I turn my eyes to him. He looks buoyant, his energy at a level high above anything I've seen from him.

Noah's fingers ease up and the scene before me blurs until it fades away. I open my eyes.

"Amanda was a second-timer," I say when I can find my voice.

"She was," Noah agrees.

"She's back in The Life-After now?"

"Yes, she is."

I'm silent for a minute, still puzzling over why she was with Riley.

"Was she assigned to Riley, too?" I ask.

"No, but they grew up together," he replies. "They were very close."

I watch his face and see a familiar expression. There's something he's waiting for me to realize, but I'm not sure what it is.

"How did she leave?"

He sits down in the chair again. "Everyone who knew her thought it was a surfing accident out in Malibu."

Malibu is where I'm supposed to be when it's my time to go back. Another ocean accident. I wonder if her accident was made to look like she'd been caught in a riptide, just like my accident is supposed to appear.

"Was he with her?" I ask.

"No. He was working that morning at the studio. He planned to meet her later on in the day so they could surf together."

"Anything else I should know?"

I don't expect an answer, but I find my eyes closing from a force not my own.

18

⸺ • ⸺

CHAPTER 18

Images of Riley flash in front of me again. I see him arriving at the beach, a surfboard in his arms. He heads toward a bluff, scanning the surf and the sand for someone. I'm pretty sure he's looking for Amanda. As he gets closer, though, he can see a crowd of people in a circle around something that's blocked from his view. When he gets behind them, he rises up on the balls of his feet to get a look at what's happening, and then he's crumpling to his knees. The noise that escapes his lips is something I've only heard once before, when I was Anna. It came from me when I realized David had disappeared.

I fight to open my eyes but they're glued shut. Next is the funeral. What I can see of the service is mostly blurry, and it's clear my attention is being called to Riley. He sits in the front row of the church, gripping the hand of a woman who might be Amanda's mother. There's anguish there, but it's muted now, like he's found the sweetly numbing embrace that only shock can give. There's something else, though, and it burns brighter in his energy than the anguish or even the grief. It takes me a second or two to zero in on it. When I do, my eyes fly open.

It's a struggle to breathe as I come back to my senses. I feel as though I want to crawl out of my skin until Noah puts a hand on my shoulder and I'm flooded with a sense of calm.

"He feels guilty about Amanda?" I ask, once I find my voice again.

"He thinks he could have saved her if he'd left the studio earlier instead of staying a few extra minutes to talk with the band." Okay, simple enough.

Noah's not done, though. "Did you see anything else in his energy?" he asks.

I shake my head, since it was obvious what was going on with Riley at the funeral. "The guilt was overriding pretty much everything."

"Look closer this time."

I close my eyes and wait until I see Riley again, still at the funeral. He's staring at Amanda's casket, but I don't look at that. Instead, I watch the sparks of guilt still in his energy and then focus in closer, until I understand what Noah means. Something isn't right with the color, and this isn't just guilt. I pick an energy spark to study more closely. The spark jumps closer to me, magnified like I have it under a microscope. This close, it seems to split into other pieces and I look at the color and vibration of each one. There's something familiar about this, something I've seen before in another vision. It was a vision of me as Anna, when I saw what happened to my energy in the week before I died.

"The color," I whisper. "What is that?"

My eyes are still closed as I watch the pinks and deep reds dance together, rolling over one another and then becoming muted and brightening again. The spark glows like a fiery ember, so bright I think it might burn me if I reach out to touch it.

"I think you know," I hear Noah say.

I want to tell him that if I knew, I wouldn't be asking him. I don't, though, because I learned a long time ago he doesn't budge when he thinks there's something I need to figure out for myself. I keep watching, wondering what it could mean, until a thought forms in my mind that makes my eyes open again.

"Riley and Amanda were a lot more than close friends, weren't they?" The words tumble out of my mouth as a question, even though I know the answer from what I've just seen. I feel myself pitch sideways, the reason for why I'm here slamming into me fast and hard. I grab on to the side of my bed.

"Yes." Noah watches me closely as I steady myself.

"How much more?" I demand. I can't be hearing what I'm hearing, and especially not when he seems so casual about it.

"He thought he'd marry her after they finished college."

"Riley fell in love with a second-timer?" I stare at him so long and so hard that for the first time I can remember, he looks away first.

"Yes."

"The Life-After let him fall in love with her?" He has to be kidding me. If it were possible for steam to come out of my ears and nostrils, I'm pretty sure that would be happening right now. Noah must sense it, because he finally looks at me.

"It's not the same thing as you and David." He knows exactly where I'm heading with this.

"How is it any different?" My voice is shrill, but I can't help it. Noah's lucky that my aunt is in the house and I can't do what I really feel like doing, which would involve a lot of yelling.

He opens his mouth to speak, but I cut him off. "An innocent in The Before crosses paths with someone from The Life-After who wasn't sent here to help him, falls in love, and is devastated when that person is just gone one day? Does that sound like any other life you might know? Some other cosmic accident, perhaps?"

"Are you done?" Noah asks. His voice is quiet. I glare at him, and he takes it as a signal to continue. "What happened to Riley won't end up as a cosmic accident as long as you do what you're here for."

I bring my thumb and forefinger up to pinch the bridge of my nose. This is crazy, but I don't say anything.

Noah continues. "Amanda was different from David, because she didn't stay past her time. She was here to help someone else, and she left when she was supposed to. Her path was always going to cross with Riley's."

"And you were always going to let Riley fall in love with her," I add.

"You can't help who falls in love with you, or who you fall in love with. Of anyone, I think you know that. That's why you were sent here years ago to help Riley now. We don't have to cut his life short if you do your part. But if you don't, he won't ever get back on track and his energy won't be ready for The Life-After. He'll have to die and come back as a second-timer." He tries to hold my eyes, but I look past him to my bedroom window.

"So what do you want me to do?" I watch a leaf stir on a tree outside.

"Do you remember the dead spot in your energy?"

It takes a lot of willpower not to snort at his question. Of course I do.

I turn my gaze away from the window and back to him. "I'd almost forgotten about why I'm here, but thanks for reminding me."

If he hears the sarcasm in my voice, he ignores it. "You're here to keep that from happening to Riley, so he can move forward to have the life he's meant for."

"And that means what, exactly?"

"It's your job to help him open his heart again. He needs to, or this will turn into a cosmic accident for him. Just like with you."

Just like me. What a disaster.

I fold my arms across my chest. "If I'm the one who makes that happen, though, wouldn't that mean he's opening his heart to me?"

Noah is silent for long enough to make me nervous. Finally, he speaks.

"That's exactly what it means. This is your mission here."

"To make him love me so then I can go and die on him, too? Don't you think that's going to be a problem?" I feel an ache starting at my temples. I don't know if it's from my energy being low tonight, or if it's from having to think about all of this.

"Are you questioning your mission and the wisdom of The Life-After?" he asks.

"You'd better believe I am."

"Then I'd advise you to stop doing that."

He's actually serious. I can't imagine how he believes Riley will be able to handle my death like it's absolutely nothing if he opens his heart to me. This is going to be a cosmic accident either way.

"This is insane," I tell him. "You can't ask me to do this, just so I can leave him to grieve again. It doesn't even make sense."

Noah picks up his hat and places it back on his head. "It might not from what you can see, but it does. Just trust. This is your job."

I open my mouth to argue that my job is to help Riley, not destroy him, but Noah is already gone.

"Coward," I mutter, even though I'm talking to my bed. I can't believe this is happening.

What I'm being asked to do to Riley is something I wouldn't wish upon my greatest enemy. He's already lost someone he was in love with once, which is one more time than anyone should have to experience it without knowing about The Life-After and all that comes next.

19

CHAPTER 19

Countdown to The Life-After: four weeks.

"Where's my phone?"

I haven't said a word to my aunt in the last three days. The secret has been ducking out of the house as early as possible for Amarleen's class in the morning, and making sure I'm in whatever room my aunt isn't in when we're both at home. I'd be on my way to my yoga class right now, except my phone went missing from my bedroom some time between when I got into the shower and when I got out. I know exactly who has it, and the look of sweetness and innocence on my aunt's face tells me I'm right.

"I'm sure it's wherever you left it," she tells me. "You should really be more careful with your things."

"Stealing my phone is theft. That's against the law, if you didn't know."

She walks over to the cupboard and pulls out two mugs. "I don't know what you're talking about. Would you like some coffee, and maybe we can talk about what you'll need for school? It's just a few weeks until you start."

"Keep living in your dream world."

I turn on my heel and walk out of the kitchen, grabbing my yoga mat and purse from where I left them in the hallway. I guess I'm heading out for the day without my phone. My aunt probably thinks if I can't text or get phone calls, then she's cut me off from boys or anyone else I know here. In her mind, this will somehow make it easier to get me on a plane and back to the plans she has for my life. I'm certainly not going to tell her I can just go buy a new one and reactivate my number and all of my contacts and text messages. I don't want to know what level she'd stoop to after that.

I slam the door behind me and walk down the driveway to my car. The drive to my yoga class should put me in a better mood. Then I just have to figure out how to stay away from my house for as long as possible, preferably until my aunt is asleep. There has to be a way to get her out of here that doesn't involve me being with her on a plane to Boston.

I get to Diamond Lotus Yoga earlier than I usually do. Another class with a different teacher is still finishing up in the classroom. Selena is at the front desk, getting a new student set up. Even though I look away from her as quickly as possible, I can feel her eyes boring into me.

I turn my head and pretend to look at a spot to the left of the desk, and that's when I see Amarleen. She's watching Selena and me. I smile at her and then have to move my eyes to something else. If I don't, she'll see everything I'm feeling and maybe even everything I've done. Maybe she already does. She can hear my thoughts right now if she wants to, after all. I try hard not to squirm.

My eyes land on the bathroom door. It's a temporary escape, anyway. I head for the door, smiling again at Amarleen as I pass by. I don't realize I'm holding my breath until I'm through the door and it closes behind me. Exhale. I set my rolled-up yoga mat on a chair in the corner and then look at myself in the mirror hanging above the sinks. Wow. There's a girl who doesn't look happy and who sure isn't hiding it.

The bathroom door squeaks as it swings open. In the mirror's reflection I see Selena standing behind me, staring at the back of my head.

"What were you doing with Riley?" she asks, meeting my eyes in the mirror. She doesn't look happy, either. At least I'm in good company.

"Hanging out," I say, turning around to look at her.

"You should stop doing that."

"Why would I do that?"

"Because he needs friends in his life, and people who know how to care."

"I care about him."

"Fat chance of that," she mutters. I pretend not to hear her and focus in on her energy instead. I expect to see sparks of anger, but instead see colors of protection.

"Are you close with him?" I try to sound casual. What I'd give to be able to read her thoughts right now.

"We've been friends since I moved here," she replies, dropping her eyes to study something on the floor.

I can't tell if she's ever felt more than friendship toward Riley, but I don't see jealousy or anything like it in her energy. There's just that fierce protectiveness. Selena would shield a good friend from anything, I know. Well, she would unless that friend betrayed her, like I did.

She moves her eyes back up, fixing them on me. "He's a good guy. And he's been through enough without dealing with you."

I know she means Amanda. I also know what she means about dealing with me.

The last time we spoke to each other, it was in the garden behind her parents' house on the night of her family's going-away party. Selena had been miserable for weeks, ever since her dad announced he'd been made a partner at his law firm and was being transferred to the firm's new office in L.A. She was sad about leaving Boston, and sad about leaving our school and starting over somewhere else as the new girl, but it was absolutely destroying her to be leaving me. We'd been joined at the hip since my aunt and uncle took me in, doing everything together as best-friends-forever for over nine years.

So I avoided her the last two weeks she lived in Boston. Didn't answer her calls at home. Ducked out during lunch at school, when we'd always sat together in the cafeteria. Pretended I didn't hear her when she called after me in the hall, and didn't look at her in the classes we had together. Stopped answering notes she left at my locker. Pretended to always be hanging out with Delilah James, another girl we knew from school, and purposely didn't invite her to hang out with us. Radio silence.

I hadn't planned on going to her family's going-away party. My aunt made me, though. Not through threats of being grounded or taking some privilege away, either. She took me by the arm, hauled me into the bathroom and styled my hair, and then refused to budge from outside the door until I put on the dress she picked out for me. I think she would have put one of those toddler leashes on me if she could have. I was sullen for the short walk two doors over to the Jensen's house, but plastered a smile on my face when Mr. and Mrs. Jensen let us inside. After that I did everything I could to dodge Selena, at one point escaping outside to a part of the backyard where nobody seemed to be. I slipped into the garden as quietly as I could, hoping the tall hedges would let me go undetected for at least the next half hour.

I sat down on the garden swing, watching the stars and the quarter-moon in the sky and trying to ignore the chill in the night air. It wasn't long before I heard footsteps. Selena was in front of me before I could get up from the swing.

"Why are you avoiding me?" Her hands were folded across her chest and she tried to sound like she was angry, but everything about her told me she was sad. More than sad, actually. Her energy was too heavy for me to look at for more than a second or two. I tried not to flinch and pushed away the pang of guilt as best as I could. I did this to her, I knew. And I had to keep doing it.

"I'm not avoiding you. I just wanted to come outside for a while. Is that a crime?"

My voice was cool and sharp, not at all the tone Selena was used to hearing from me. She blinked, hard.

"I didn't mean here," she said, her voice sounding strained. She was barely keeping it together. I studied the stones paving the garden pathway. "I meant at school, and every time I've tried to call you. Where have you been?"

"With Delilah."

I watched Selena bite her lip. She thought that was the truth, and that Delilah had replaced her in my life almost instantly. She didn't know that as soon as she was on her way to L.A., I'd stop hanging out with Delilah, too. It was better not to let anyone get too close.

"Why are you hanging out with Delilah so much?" she asked. She sounded so small that all I wanted to do was hug her, but I shrugged instead and looked up at the night sky.

"She's my friend. That's what friends do."

"I thought we were friends, though." Selena's lip started to quiver. I felt a lump the size of a grapefruit form in my throat and swallowed hard. I couldn't let her know this was killing me just as much as it was killing her.

"We were," I said. I hoped Selena hadn't heard the catch in my voice.

"We aren't anymore?" She folded her arms a little more tightly across her chest.

"You're moving to L.A."

"That doesn't mean we have to stop being friends, or that it's okay for you to replace me. You could at least wait until I'm gone to find a new best friend."

I'd hurt her, but it still wasn't enough for her to stop wanting to be friends with me. I had to change that. It was for her own good.

"Look, you think you're all broken up about moving thousands of miles away, but what about me? Everything for the last few weeks has been all about you, you, you, and how moving is ruining your life. You haven't even asked how I feel. That tells me what kind of friend you are."

"What?" She couldn't have looked more stunned if I'd slapped her.

"You've just been so selfish, self-centered, and self-absorbed. Think about someone else for a change. Not everything is about you."

"Do you even hear what you're saying?"

"Do you?" I asked her.

She didn't know what to say to that. I saw tears well up in her eyes and knew I couldn't stay to see her cry. I'd crumble if I did, so I got up from the swing.

"I hope you have a good move to L.A."

I didn't wait for her to answer. Turning my back to her, I walked away as fast as I could. She didn't follow me.

The girl who stood in front of me that night was devastated. The girl standing in front of me now in the bathroom at Diamond Lotus Yoga is angry, and rightfully so.

"I'm Riley's friend," I tell her.

"No, you're not." She shakes her head. "You don't even know what the word means. I should know, after all."

I don't have an answer for that. The night of her family's going-away party, I'd been prepared with what to say. This is a surprise attack. My silence doesn't matter, though, because Selena keeps talking.

"I don't know what you're doing here, or why Amarleen hasn't seen right through you. But if you hurt Riley even a little bit, you won't be coming back here and you'll wish you'd never met me."

It's two years of anger and hurt coming out of her, and I know she isn't kidding. She gives me one last look before she turns around and stalks out of the bathroom. The door closes behind her. I stare at it, knowing I deserve every bit of fury Selena has for me.

I'd be lying if I said I don't miss her friendship. I loved Selena like a sister, and I still do. That's why I had to put distance between us and make her think I didn't want us to be friends anymore. This way, she won't miss me as much when I'm gone. Maybe she won't miss me at all.

Class is harder than I expected it to be. The exercises are tough, and every time I think my energy is getting stronger, I close my eyes and see Selena standing in front of me, shooting daggers with her eyes.

I can tell there's something Amarleen wants to say to me from the way she watches me after class. The lineup of people waiting to talk to her is long, though, and I want to be alone right now. The last thing I feel like doing is talking about what's going on with my energy today, or about what Amarleen might have seen going on between Selena and me by the front desk before class.

I think about ordering a green tea from the Diamond Lotus Yoga café and then sitting outside on the patio for a while. I head for the counter and spot Selena standing at the front of the line. She takes a mug from the cashier and heads away from the counter, toward the door that leads to the patio. There goes that plan. One round with Selena today was enough. I guess I'll get my green tea to go.

I don't want to go home, but with Selena occupying the patio and Riley working in the studio today, I can't think of anywhere else to go while I'm still in yoga clothes. So I take the long way home, driving up winding side roads in the Hollywood Hills until I'm on my street and pulling into my driveway.

I suck in my breath as I walk up to the front door, waiting for my aunt to pounce the second I'm inside. Then I turn the door handle. Nothing. I let out the breath and put my yoga mat down in the corner of the foyer, then head for the kitchen.

I stop outside of the kitchen entrance, poking my head around the corner. My aunt isn't in the room, but I can see her through the window. She's outside sitting beside the pool, her cell phone pressed against her ear, and she probably doesn't know I'm home. With any luck, she won't realize it for a while.

I tiptoe out of the kitchen and head down the hallway to the bedroom she's set up camp in, glancing around the room for any sign of my phone. It's not on the bed or the dresser, so I open the closet door. My aunt's clothes fill the closet, hanging neatly on hangers, and her shoes are lined up along the floor. To look at this, you would think she's moved in permanently. I know this means she's not budging. Aunt Sarah is nothing if not stubborn. Wonderful.

I reach for the handle of one of her suitcases and know I'm on the right track when I hear something roll around inside. I pull it out of the closet and unzip it, and there's my phone. It's the only thing inside. I reach in and grab it, then zip up the suitcase and roll it back into the closet.

It's a good thing my phone is password-protected so she couldn't do any serious damage. Holding it in my hand, I walk out of the room and head for my bedroom. I'll just have to hide my phone or lock it up somewhere until I figure out how to make my aunt leave.

One thing is clear. The few weeks I have left in The Before will just be harder with my aunt around, especially if she tries to block me from seeing or talking to Riley. The woman has to go.

20

CHAPTER 20

The morning is already ridiculously warm when I wake up. There's a note on the kitchen table from my aunt telling me she's gone for a spa day at some place in Beverly Hills that I'm sure she'll find everything wrong with. Good. This means I'm wearing her down.

Not enough, though. The note warns me she'll be back in time for dinner. Guess I'll have to try harder. I can think about how I'm going to do that while I sit by the pool, loving her absence and the hot weather. After changing into a bikini, I grab a towel, a book, and some sunscreen, and then I head outside.

I get in about twenty minutes of reading before a text message alert pulls me out of the story and back into the real world. I pick up my phone. It's a message from Riley.

Did you know nothing rhymes with the word "orange"?

I shake my head. I know he's supposed to be filling in for the receptionist at his parents' studio all this week, but he can't be busy if he's pondering rhymes.

Slacker. Boring day at the studio? Send.

My phone chimes again. Nope. Boring morning writing lyrics.

You aren't working? Weird. I send the message. It's about a minute before I get another text.

Riley: Laryngitis. Can't answer the phone when people call, and can't answer any questions anyone at the studio has for me without writing everything down. Got kicked out by my mom.

Me: How'd you lose your voice? Are you sick?

Riley: Nope, blew out my voice singing. The doc says not to use my voice at all for the next 36 hours.

Me: Yikes.

Riley: It's harder than you'd think. I'm getting good at being a mime.

Me: I'll bet. So does this mean you're going to text me all day?

Riley: Pretty much. What are you doing?

Me: Hanging out at my pool. Want to join me?

Riley: I can't use my voice.

Me: You're right. Sitting by a pool definitely requires screaming at the top of your lungs. Karaoke, too.

Riley: You and your sarcasm.

Me: You know I'm right. It's 92 degrees.

Riley: You're right that it's 92 degrees.

Me: So why are you sitting in your apartment and texting me when you could be outside sitting by a pool and probably still texting me from right beside me?

Riley: It's the principle of the thing.

Me: Don't say I didn't offer when you're melting this afternoon.

Riley: Be there in half an hour.

I set my phone down on the lounge chair, catching sight of my reflection on the screen. I'm smiling. I guess I do that when I win.

I keep reading until the heat makes me feel like it's entirely possible I'll melt into my chair. Pool time. I get up and jump into the water, feet first. Just as my head starts to go underwater, I hear my phone chime. Once I'm back above the surface, I swim over to the side of the pool and hoist myself out.

I read the message from Riley. I'm in your driveway. I can't really yell for you.

Droplets of water fall from my hair onto the screen. I reach for a towel to dry myself off. My hair still dripping wet, I walk across the sundeck and into the house, making my way to the front door. I'm suddenly aware of how little of me my bikini covers, and that Riley's never seen me anything but fully clothed. Not that I know why this matters. It must be the heat. Still, I wrap the towel around my waist before opening the door.

Riley waves and smiles. There's total silence, which makes me laugh.

"You not being able to talk could be a lot of fun," I tell him. He waggles his eyebrows at me and steps inside of the house. "The pool's that way," I say, pointing him in the direction of the door to the backyard. "I'll get you a towel and meet you out there."

I walk down the hallway and grab a beach towel from the linen closet. When I get back outside, I stop so fast I nearly trip over the tops of my flip-flops. The hand that's not holding the towel shoots out to grab onto the doorframe behind me. Smooth. Here's hoping I don't look like a complete klutz. Riley doesn't seem to notice, though. How could he when he's sprawled out on a lounge chair, shirtless, his nose buried in my trashy romance novel? Awesome. I should have hidden that somewhere.

I can't really think too much about the book, though. Not when I realize I've never seen him without a shirt on before. That's probably a really good thing, since I'm having a hard time keeping my jaw in place. Holy cow.

He holds the book up and catches me mid-stare. I feel heat rising to my face. He points at the book cover, smirking, and I know that I have to be turning bright red. Let's hope he thinks it's because he's discovered that I don't always like to read about string theory.

"It's not like you can read about anything serious outside in the sun," I scoff, tossing his towel at him. It lands on his face.

He puts the towel beside him on the chair, and then picks up his phone and waves it at me.

"Words with Friends?" I ask. It's the only phone game I can think of.

He shakes his head and starts typing something. A moment later, I hear my phone's text message alert.

Read to me? Looks like a hot book.

I glance over at him. He contorts his face into a suggestive look. I don't know what color you turn after your face is already on fire, but I'm sure Riley is finding out right now. Curse him.

Just be cool, I tell myself. That should be easy. This is Riley, after all, and we're friends. I'm here to help him, not make out with him. Well, not unless I listen to Noah, and that's not high up on my list of things to do right now.

"What, does that kind of thing turn you on?" I flip a few strands of my wet hair over my shoulder. I can be indifferent. No problem.

He nods, keeping the suggestive look on his face. There's a little flutter in my stomach and then I catch myself. I'm being silly, and I'm going to put an end to this right now.

I get up from my chair. "Read to you, hmm?" I walk over to him and stop beside his chair. I keep my eyes on him when I lean in close. I could be wrong, but I swear I see his eyes widen. Good. A flushed face would be better, but whatever. Then I grab the book from his hand. "In your dreams."

I saunter back to my chair and toss my book beside it. Then I turn around and give him a wicked grin.

"It's kind of fun that you can't talk," I say. He gives me a look that clearly says, Oh really?

He swings his legs over the side of his chair and gets up. I eye him, but it looks like he's heading for the pool. I look away for a second to grab the bottle of sunscreen and when I look up again, he's at my side. Before I know what's happening, he's scooping me up from my chair and holding me against his chest, his face only inches from mine.

"Um, what are you doing?" I swear his face is getting closer, and my heart starts to get a little crazy. Yup. We're almost nose-to-nose. Then I see we're at the edge of the pool, and I realize what he's up to.

"Don't you dare," I growl. He smiles a very innocent-looking smile. Then he dangles me over the pool and lets go. Water splashes around me as my feet hit the surface of the pool, followed by the rest of me.

The water is nice compared to the heat, but I'm not telling him that. I try to glare at him, but it's impossible not to laugh.

"You're in so much trouble," I declare between giggles.

He widens his eyes and points to himself, as if saying, Who, me?

"Yes, you," I answer, taking slow steps across the pool floor. He winks and sits down at the pool's edge, his legs hanging down into the water. He's probably convinced there's no way I can try to get back at him since he's bigger than me, but he's wrong. I creep closer to him and put my arms out in front of me like I'm going to grab onto the side of the pool and lift myself out. Then I reach over and yank hard on his arm, throwing him off balance. He falls into the pool with me, water splashing onto the pool deck. Good job, me.

"Guess I win," I tell him, smirking at the look he's giving me. A wall of water hits me in the face a second later, followed instantly by another wave.

"This is war," I warn him. I raise my arm to thrash water in his direction but his hand catches my wrist. His other hand grabs my other wrist, and now I can't move.

Our eyes lock. Keeping hold of both of my wrists, he moves forward until he's close enough for me to feel his breath. The look on his face is intense, and he's even closer now. I feel my eyes close.

Then my head is underwater, pushed down by the same hand that was holding one of my wrists. When I come back up, trying to get the water out of my nose without actually snorting, he's already clear across the pool.

"You're making lunch," I grumble at him, wading over to the side of the pool and pulling myself out. His grin gets bigger. "What?" I ask, putting my hands on my hips.

He shrugs and follows me out of the pool. I dry myself off with my towel while I wait for him, but then find myself showered with more drops of water when he walks right up to me and shakes out his hair.

"You're asking for it," I say, swatting him with my towel. He gives me his best puppy-dog look as I stalk off toward the house. I turn my head to face forward so he can't see that I'm smiling.

Once we get to the kitchen, I pull a head of lettuce and some other vegetables out of the fridge and put him to work making a salad. He still hasn't put a shirt on now that we're inside. I've at least wrapped my towel around my waist and the tops of my legs, though I'm not sure why. He's seen all of that uncovered outside. But something about him standing half-naked at my kitchen counter makes me self-conscious now, and maybe it's because I can't do anything other than stare at him.

He spreads his hands out over a pile of vegetables he's chopped, displaying his work for my approval. He looks up with a question on his face that disappears when he catches me staring at him. The question is replaced by a thoughtful look and slight squint of his eyes that I don't think he means for me to see. He's probably wondering what I'm looking at. That, or he wants to know why I'm not telling him how beautiful his chopped vegetables look. Or maybe it's neither of those things. I think I need to stop thinking.

"Excuse me for a second," I mumble, taking off into the hallway. I keep walking until I'm in the living room, where I left my iPod.

I'll fix this with music. If there's music, I don't have to talk. He can't talk, so this is good. We'll just listen to something, and I'll calm down enough to stop being ridiculous. Because this is beyond ridiculous, bordering on insane. He's Riley, after all. Shirt or not, flirt or not.

I take a deep breath and square my shoulders, then head back to the kitchen. When I get there, I keep my eyes off of Riley and on the stereo I'm headed for. I put my iPod into the dock and fumble for a second until I find the playlist I'm looking for, then turn up the volume. The sweet sound of music fills the room and I feel like it's safe to turn around again. Except that when I do, Riley's looking at me in a way that makes me think I've grown a second head. My heart starts to thud.

"What?" I demand.

He puts down the knife he's holding and glances around the room. I can tell when he spots what he's looking for, because he walks over to the fridge and grabs the notepad and pen that are stuck to the door. He scribbles something on the notepad and brings it over to me. I glance down at the words he's scrawled.

How do you know this band?

"Wait, do you know this band?" I ask. I downloaded the song that's playing right now after discovering the band by accident when they played the side stage at a music festival in Boston. I wasn't actually supposed to be there, but I told my aunt I'd scheduled an extra guitar lesson and got my free pass out of the house.

He nods, taking the notepad from me and writing something else.

My friend John is the drummer. That's whose side project I've been wrecking my vocal chords on.

"You're kidding?" He shakes his head and starts writing again.

They're playing a show here next week. Want to go?

"I definitely want to go," I answer. That's what slips out of my mouth before it hits me that this could be a date. No, not a date. Just a night out with a friend. Because friends do things like go to shows together. I keep telling myself that while I turn my back to him to grab a salad bowl from the cupboard, trying to ignore my racing heart.

21

CHAPTER 21

It's late afternoon when Riley heads home. I peer through the pane of glass beside the front door, watching him back out of the driveway. I make a face at him when he spots me and waves. He laughs and makes the same face back at me, and then he's at the end of the driveway, pulling onto the street.

I take a step away from the door, pausing when I notice there's a town car stopped on the street. It pulls up in front of the house and a driver gets out to open the back door. My aunt steps out. The foul look on her face tells me she saw Riley leaving. Fantastic.

When the front door of the house opens, I brace myself.

"So I was right that you're hanging out with some boy," she yells from the foyer. I don't even have to see her face to know she's angry. "Who is he?"

"Riley," I say, but I don't bother to yell like she just did. Maybe she hears me, and maybe she doesn't.

She storms into the kitchen a second later, glaring at me. I wouldn't expect anything else. Her lips are puckered together, too, which makes her look like she's swallowed a lemon. I'd point this out, but I'm pretty sure that would just make the lecture she's about to start giving me even longer. And I'm one-hundred-percent certain there's a lecture coming, because I know my aunt. She opens her mouth and I silently count down. Three, two, one.

"Young lady, there are rules about being alone with boys in the house. Maybe I wasn't clear enough since you didn't try that in Boston, but I don't believe for a second that you've forgotten what those rules are."

I'd tell her Riley isn't my boyfriend, but it doesn't seem worth it. Besides, we have something more important to clear up.

"This isn't your house," I remind her. "I'm eighteen, and this house is mine now. That means I make the rules here and not you. If you don't like it, you can leave." Please, please leave. Please.

I turn around and head outside to the pool, fully expecting her to follow me there and launch into a new lecture about respect and how little of it I have. She doesn't, though, which is not normal Aunt Sarah behavior. Not that I mind this. If she's not coming into the backyard, then I'm staying. My book is still out here where I left it beside the chair. I'll read that and try to savor the peace.

It's just before sunset when I finish the last page of my book and decide it's safe to head inside. I open the door as quietly as I can, hoping to make it to my bedroom without running into my aunt along the way. It's like being held hostage in my own house.

I only get as far as the hallway before coming to a dead stop. There, lined up against the wall, are all of my suitcases. Each one of them is bulging, which tells me all of my clothes and belongings are crammed inside. My aunt walks out of my bedroom, my airplane carry-on slung over her shoulder.

She's changed into a cream-colored linen skirt and blazer, diamond earrings dangling from her ears. Uh oh. This is a first-class-travel kind of outfit. My aunt wouldn't be caught dead wiping her hands on a hot towel and enjoying silverware and an open bar while wearing jeans and a T-shirt. I'm not sure she even owns a pair of jeans.

"Am I going somewhere?" I fold my arms over my chest. My aunt sets the carry-on down on the table in the hall.

"We're both going somewhere. I left travel clothes out for you on your bed, since you're definitely not fit to fly in that." She wrinkles her nose at the sundress I pulled on over my bathing suit earlier this afternoon.

"Where is it we're going?" I ask, even though I already know the answer.

"We have a flight out to Boston tonight." She says it like it's the most natural thing in the world to have packed up my suitcases and booked a ticket for me. It's the same way she acted when the airport limo showed up in the driveway the other day. The woman is crazy.

"Ah," I say, unfolding my arms. "Well, you enjoy that flight. Say hi to Uncle Mike for me when you get there."

She looks me up and down. I recognize the controlled expression on her face. It always shows up when we're in the middle of an argument and I do something to successfully get under her skin. One point, me.

"We're both on that flight, and I'm not leaving here without you," she replies.

"You're definitely leaving without me since I'm not going anywhere with you," I say, walking past her into the kitchen. I open the fridge and take out a bottle of water.

I hear her footsteps behind me. When the footsteps stop, I turn around to see that she's standing in the doorway. Yup, she's mad.

"We need to leave now, so go get dressed. That's an order." If it were possible, I'm sure there'd be smoke pouring out of her ears. My aunt has never been good at not getting her own way.

I unscrew the plastic cap from the top of the bottle and take a drink of my water before answering her.

"You need to leave now, not me." I set the bottle down on the counter.

She ignores me, heading back to the hallway. When I hear a scuffling noise and the sound of something rolling, I walk back across the kitchen. From the doorway, I watch my aunt roll one of my suitcases toward the front door.

"Leave that here," I warn her. She opens the door and rolls the suitcase outside. I follow her and see that there's a car waiting in the driveway. The driver steps out and reaches for the suitcase, but I wave him off.

"If you'd like a theft charge to go along with trespassing, then go ahead and put that suitcase into the car." I'm talking to my aunt, but the driver freezes with his hand in mid-air.

My threat makes my aunt stop, too. "I beg your pardon?" she asks.

"You need to leave, but you need to leave my stuff here."

"Then I'm not going." She lets go of the handle of my suitcase and puts her hands on her hips. The driver looks from her to me and back to her again.

"Maybe you didn't hear me," I say, grabbing hold of the handle on my suitcase and rolling it back to the house. "You're going, but I'm staying right here. I'm eighteen now, and I can make my own decisions."

Her heels clack on the pavement as she follows me into the house. "You're still a child. This hare-brained plan of yours to put off college just shows me that you can't be in charge of your own life."

She reaches for my suitcase again but I yank it away from her. As calmly as I can, I walk over to where she's left her own suitcases in the hallway. Taking a handle in each hand, I roll them over to her.

"Get out," I tell her. "If you don't, I'm getting someone here to get you out. It's your choice."

She narrows her eyes at me. "You wouldn't dare."

"Try me." I go back to the hallway for her carry-on, then walk past her and deposit it on the front stoop.

"Just wait until your uncle hears about this. You're coming back to Boston, and if you think dealing with me is something, wait until he comes to get you." Her face is almost purple. I know she's doing everything she can to not lose her cool in front of the driver, who's still standing speechless in the driveway. This would be a full-blown tantrum if he wasn't here.

"She's going to LAX," I call to him. "You can start the car."

"I will cut off your bank account," she growls, stomping back outside of the house.

"You haven't had access to it since I turned eighteen," I remind her. I walk past her and into the house, shutting the door before she can say anything else. I lock it behind me.

I know this is probably the last time I'll see my aunt before I return to The Life-After. If it were up to me, it wouldn't have ended this way. It's not up to me, though, and I don't have time for this. I can't go back to Boston, and I can't tell her why. But if I don't get her out of my hair so I can focus on helping Riley, he's going to die. If he dies, I'll never get back to The Life-After.

I close my eyes for a moment. When I open them again, I spot my phone on the table. I pick it up and start a new text message to my uncle.

Aunt Sarah is on her way home. You may want to get her from the airport when she gets there. I hit send.

My phone rings less than a minute later. I don't have to be psychic to know it's my uncle. Sure enough, it's his number I see on the screen.

Moving my finger to the phone's power button, I press down and watch the phone shut off. This isn't something I can deal with tonight, or maybe even before I leave this place for The Life-After.

22

—·—

Chapter 22

C ountdown to The Life-After: three weeks.

"Evening, senorita." Riley swoops down into a low bow on my front doorstep. He seems like he's in an awfully good mood.

"The frog left your throat," I comment, holding open the door. "Or did the cat let go of your tongue?"

"The doctor told me I could speak again, so brace yourself." He grins and walks inside. I close the door and lean against it, trying not to let on that I see his eyes sweeping over my face and body.

"You look incredible." His eyes hold mine.

I flush. "You look great too," I murmur, hoping I don't sound as self-conscious as I feel.

We stand there looking at each other. I can almost hear the air crackle as my energy extends out, reaching closer to his. A tiny shock runs through me and I try not to jump. There it is, the energy connection. It's like static electricity tonight. I don't realize I'm light-headed until I try to stop leaning against the door. I need a moment to get it together, someplace where he isn't.

"I just need to get my purse and then we can go," I tell him. I head for my bedroom, hoping I'm not swaying as I walk.

I come back with my purse a minute later and let him lead me out the door. I think I've managed to collect myself until my foot grazes a white feather by the side of the car. Riley doesn't seem to see it. I don't mention it to him, instead giving him a smile as he opens the passenger door for me.

When we're both inside the car and Riley starts the engine, I'm relieved to hear the stereo come to life. We drive without talking for a few minutes, listening to the music.

We're headed into Hollywood before there's a pause in the songs. It must be the end of the playlist. I look over at Riley.

"I never did ask where the show is tonight," I say.

Riley reaches for a button in the middle of the dashboard. Music fills the car again, but he turns the volume down. "Silver Lake, at a place called The Satellite. Ever been there?"

The Satellite wasn't there when I was Anna. "Nope. What is it?" I ask.

He shrugs. "A small club, lots of up-and-coming bands. I like it there."

We drive until I see fewer big buildings on the sides of the street, and more houses. We circle a few of the streets near The Satellite before we find a spot to park.

Once we're inside of The Satellite, we stop at the box office. Riley tells the woman behind the counter that we're on a list and gives her our names. She scans a piece of paper in front of her and then hands each of us a yellow bracelet.

Riley reaches down to grab my hand and leads me to another door that he opens for both of us. I try not to let him catch me looking down at our hands. There are a whole lot of sparks dancing where our fingers are joined, and I'm feeling every one of them.

Shadows linger in every corner inside the bar, with only a hint of light coming from the empty stage and a glassed-in area at the back of the room. By the stage, tiny white lights hang over silver and blue curtains. I think they're going for an outer space vibe, if outer space looked a little bit like the 1970s. Not so many points for the other-worldly experience, but I'm probably just picky about that. I know what other-worldly is like.

I see Riley watching me as we walk farther into bar. Probably wondering if this is my style, I think.

You think wrong. It's Noah's voice I hear. Wonderful. I have a chaperone. Leave it to him to read and answer my thoughts right now.

I didn't exactly invite you along on my da— I stop before I complete the word in my mind and correct myself. I didn't invite you to come with us.

You mean on your date with Riley. I can tell Noah is trying hard not to laugh.

It's not a date.

That's not what he thinks. And just so you're clear, he's watching you now because it matters to him that you have a good time tonight.

"Do you want something to drink?" Riley waves a hand in front of my face when I don't answer. I swat it away.

"Yeah. The bottle of scotch back there will do." I jerk my chin toward the bartender. I manage to keep a straight face for about all of two seconds until I hear Riley laugh.

"I'd like to see what would happen after a few shots of that," he comments.

"Oh would you?" I challenge him. "Any special reason?" I'm baiting him, but somehow I can't help myself.

Hints of pink creep into Riley's cheeks and I choke back a laugh. As his face gets brighter, I feel a whoosh of energy coming at me in a wave. It makes me a little dizzy and I wonder what it is, until I focus in on my energy and see the intense dance his energy is having with mine. Little gold and pink sparks pop up in the space where our energy meets. This is even stronger than it was a few minutes ago.

He clears his throat. "I just meant that you'll probably be a lightweight, given how tiny you are." He stares straight ahead at the bar, by all appearances examining the bottles on the shelves that line the back wall. I have a feeling he can't look at me.

"Any particular train of thought I should follow about what me being a lightweight would mean?" If I could, I'd do a double-take at myself. Since when do I flirt? That's something Anna did.

This is a bad idea, I remind myself. I wait for Noah to chime in and tell me this is exactly what I'm supposed to be doing, but he's suspiciously silent.

"Choose your own adventure," Riley tells me. A wicked grin lights up his face for just a second, but then he seems to think about what he's saying and the grin disappears. Great. He clearly needs to stop thinking.

"What does that mean?" I ask. He's looking at the bottles behind the bar again, though, and pretends not to hear me. Hmm. Let's try something else. "You're probably right, you know."

That grabs his attention. "I'm right about something?"

"Don't let it go to your head. Even broken clocks are right twice a day."

"That sounds a little more like the Cassidy I know. So what'll it be?"

"Soda water with lemon."

"Let's make that two," he says. He lets go of my hand and steps up to the bar. I stay rooted in place, watching him talk to the bartender. Our energy is still connected but it feels a little less intense with his hand no longer holding mine. I know that it's all in my mind, though, because I can see how strongly our energy is now woven together. It stays as strong as it was when we were holding hands, and it might even be getting stronger.

I walk up beside him at the bar just as he pulls his phone out from his jacket pocket and starts to type. I can't tell if he even notices that I'm beside him again. I could pull out my phone and do the same, but I'm not really sure who I'd text. Not knowing what else to do, I pretend to look around the bar again. I'm awkward at the best of times, but being on a date seems to bring this to a completely new level.

Told you so. There's Noah again.

Not a date, I correct myself.

Whatever you say, he tells me, and he sounds more than amused. Curse him.

It takes about thirty more seconds to run out of things to look at, so I turn my head back to Riley. He notices me this time and looks up from his phone.

"I'm just texting John to tell him we're here."

I nod, silently thanking the bartender when he appears in front of us and sets two glasses of soda water down on top of the counter. Riley pulls his wallet out from his back pocket and puts a few bills down on the counter. I wonder if I should be offering to pay for my drink, or the tip at least, since this isn't a date—is it?

Not a word, Noah, I think, before he can chime in with his opinion again.

Riley's fingers brush against mine and I nearly jump at the little tingles of energy when he takes my hand.

23

———— • ————

CHAPTER 23

It's a good thing my glass of soda water is still on top of the bar, since I probably would have dropped it if I'd been holding it.

Breathe, I remind myself, focusing on getting air in and out of my lungs.

"Want to sit down at a table?" Riley asks. "I think John's band is on second, so we have a while."

I nod, not trusting my voice quite yet. I'm steady enough to pick up my glass from the counter, though, and to walk the few steps it takes to get to a table.

"When you go out with me, we go out in style," he smirks, examining the top of his stool before sitting down. I check my stool before sitting, too.

"This is a lot like a place in Boston where I used to go to see bands play." I raise the straw in my glass to my lips and take a drink.

"Did you go to a lot of shows when you lived there?"

"Only when I could find a way to sneak out of my aunt and uncle's house without them catching on to where I was going. My aunt wasn't a fan of me going to any concerts that weren't someone's piano recital or a night at the opera."

"Are you sure she wasn't just concerned about you being out somewhere that wasn't safe?"

I shake my head. "If it was anyone but my aunt, I might agree with you." I take another drink, sucking the soda water through my straw a little too quickly. Bubbles fizz in my mouth, making my eyes water. I try not to cough.

"I'll learn how to drink one of these days," I manage to sputter, wiping my eyes.

"I'm trying to picture you with a tequila shot," he says. Ah, we're back to this. That didn't take long.

"It would probably be a disaster," I tell him. He looks like he wants to disagree, and I can see mischief in the golden flecks in his eyes, but he takes my lead and veers away from where I think he was going with that.

"Did you like it in Boston?" he asks.

"It was okay," I answer. "I spent most of my life there, so mostly it was just familiar." I stir the ice cubes in my glass with my straw. "Have you ever been out there?"

"Where, Boston?"

"Boston, or the northeast."

"New York City is about it," he replies. "I went out there in my senior year, thinking I might go to college there. I wanted to see what it was all about."

"Did your parents take you?"

He shakes his head. "No. I went with..." His voice trails off, and I don't know if he realizes he's stopped mid-sentence or that he has a really strange look on his face. A few moments pass before he shakes himself out of it and starts talking again. "I went with a good friend," he finishes, looking down at his glass.

He went to New York with Amanda. It doesn't take a genius to figure that out. Leave it to me to ask the ultimate mood-killing question. Not that there is a mood, or is there?

Shut it, Noah, I think, before my chaperone can chime in. He does as he's told.

I look down at my glass, too, studying the ice cubes. There are probably tons of questions I could ask Riley right now to get him to stop thinking about Amanda, but not a single one comes to mind. I move my eyes away from the ice cubes and glance at the floor.

There's a white feather on the ground beside my stool—the second one I've seen tonight. My hand shoots out to grip the side of the table. I feel Riley's hand on my back, trying to steady me.

"Careful of these stools," he warns. "They're a little wobbly."

He thinks I'm gripping the table because I'm off-balance. I tear my eyes away from the feather and give him a grateful smile.

"Thanks," I say. "Now what was that about not being a knight in shining armor?"

"Guess I should watch myself," he replies, but I can see his lips curving upward. His hand is still on my back, and I can tell we both realize it at the same time. He moves his hand away and lets it drop to his side. I take my straw between my fingers and stir the ice cubes in my glass again, watching them spin around in circles.

When I look up, I see someone watching us from across the room. He looks vaguely familiar. He starts walking toward us a second later.

"Riley, my man," he calls out as he gets closer. Riley turns around.

"Hey, man." This must be John, and now I know that where I've seen him before is on a stage in Boston. I like him already for his excellent timing.

The guy reaches his hand across the table. "Hi, I don't think we've met. I'm John."

"Cassidy," I say, shaking his hand. "I've seen you play once before, in Boston."

"Boston, huh?" he asks. I nod. "What brings you to L.A.? Are you visiting Riley?" He shoots Riley a look that plainly accuses him of keeping some sort of secret from him. Riley keeps his eyes on me.

"No, I moved out here a few weeks ago. We met when I was out one night."

The look on John's face doesn't change, but Riley still isn't looking at him. Finally, John turns back to me.

"It's great to meet you, Cassidy," he says, just as I hear a dinging sound. John reaches into his back pocket and pulls out his phone. He reads something on the screen, then looks up at us. "If you guys will excuse me for a moment, it looks like I forgot to put someone on the list. I'll let you guys get back to your date."

There's that word again. It's contagious or something, I swear. I look at Riley in time to see his face flush again, but neither of us makes any mention of the d-word. A cymbal crashes from the stage, and both of us turn to see the first band getting ready to start.

"Want to head over there?" He jerks his thumb in the direction of the stage. I nod and pick up my glass from the table.

We find a place to stand that's a few rows back and close to the wall. Riley stands behind me, and I feel a now-familiar tingle when his hand comes to rest on my shoulder a few songs into the set. By the time John's band takes the stage, I'm so close to him that I can feel his chest against my back, his chin brushing the top of my head. Anyone watching us probably thinks we're a couple.

I turn around when John's band finishes, intending to ask Riley if he wants to stick around for whatever band is on next. Some of my hair catches on his chin, though, and is pulled in front of my face. I'm about to bring my hand up to move it away when his fingers reach out, tucking my hair behind my ears. His thumb comes to rest against my jawbone. It's not a tingle I feel this time, but more like an entire swarm of butterflies in my stomach.

One day you're going to kiss me, I think. Or I at least think the words are only in my head until I see the startled look on Riley's face. I quickly turn my head away from him.

About a minute passes and neither of us says anything. I chance a quick glance at him. He seems very interested in the empty stage in front of us.

"I need to use the restroom," I mumble, sidestepping him and bolting for the back of the club.

The bathroom is small and crowded with a line of women waiting to use one of the two stalls. I stay there as long as I possibly can. Staring at myself in the mirror while washing my hands, I see that I even look like I'm panicking. I don't know what I should say when I get back to Riley, so I decide I won't say anything. I'll just pretend those words about him kissing me never came out of my mouth, and he'll do the same. We'll go home. It will be that simple, because it has to be.

After I finish drying my hands, I squeeze past the line of women by the door and head back to Riley. He's still standing where I left him in front of the stage.

"You just missed John," he tells me, once I'm beside him. "He was here for a few minutes, but then he had to go settle up with the club owner."

"Okay." It's the only intelligible word I can get out of my mouth. I twist my hands together. I'd give almost anything for pockets to jam them into right now. So much for playing it cool and acting normal.

"Ready to go?" he asks.

"Lead the way," I reply. Three words are better than one, so that's progress at least.

Riley doesn't say much on the short walk to his car, and neither do I. He opens the passenger door for me and I'm about to get in, when he puts a hand on my shoulder and stops me. I should have known I wouldn't be getting off that easily. I turn around to face him, since I know I don't really have a choice.

He keeps his hand on my shoulder. "You were right, you know." His voice is so quiet that I'm barely able to hear him.

"About what?"

"That one day, I'm going to kiss you." His thumb brushes against my cheek and he smiles, but I can see sadness in his eyes and in his energy. I try to smile back but find myself frozen in place until his hands drop to his sides.

I get into the car. I'm having trouble getting words to move past the lump that's rising in my throat. It doesn't matter, though, because once Riley closes my door and walks around the front of the car, it's like it never happened. As soon as he's behind the wheel, he reaches for the volume button on the car stereo and any thoughts I might have had are drowned out by a band I don't know. He sings along with the unfamiliar songs for the entire drive to my house.

By the time we pull into my driveway, I'm almost convinced that what happened at The Satellite took place only in my imagination. Riley certainly gives no hints that he's given it another thought since we started driving, and that's fine by me. He shifts the car into park and gets out, coming around to open my door for me. I'm left with only a quick hug before he tells me goodnight and gets back into the car. I don't know if he stays to watch me walk up the driveway, because I don't look back.

It takes me three tries to slide my key into the lock on my front door before it finally goes in. As I fumble with turning the doorknob, I realize just how much I wish that one day had been tonight.

24

CHAPTER 24

"**W**hat is wrong with me?"

I kick my shoes into a corner in the foyer and drop my purse on the floor. The question repeats over and over again in my mind as I walk into the living room and collapse onto the sofa. Letting Riley get attached to me is a disastrous idea on its own, seeing as I'm going to up and die on him in three weeks. It would be bad enough to leave it at that, but no, I have to go and let myself fall for him, too. And not just the silent, pine-from-afar-crush kind of falling for him. Oh no. I have to blurt out something that tells him exactly what I'm feeling, because that's going to make it easier when I'm gone.

"I am beyond hope," I mutter. The way my words bounce along the walls, it's as though the room agrees with me. Terrific.

I'm also tired. No, make that exhausted. Scratch that. Depleted. I am entirely depleted and having a hard time believing this isn't all some horrible mistake. I let my eyes close and lean my head against a throw pillow on the sofa.

"None of this is a mistake."

My eyes pop open when I hear Noah's voice. He's sitting in the antique armchair in the corner, holding his fedora in his hands and fighting a smile. He's smiling? Not cool.

"I don't remember inviting you to my pity party." I sit up again, grabbing the throw pillow and hugging it close to my chest.

"I don't recall it being acceptable for a higher being to have one," he says.

"If you're looking for a higher being, she's lost somewhere in the middle of a complete catastrophe."

He sets his fedora down on the table beside the armchair. "What makes you think that?"

There's nothing else to think. I'm falling for Riley and he knows it. It's hard enough for me to admit it to myself, let alone Noah, and I can't quite get the words to form on my lips. I don't need to, though. Noah is reading my thoughts.

"Why is that a bad thing?" he asks. "It's good for you to open yourself up and feel again. You know as well as I do that it's been a long time."

"Because he knows," I answer. If I hold the throw pillow any tighter, I'll probably rip it open.

"And?" He tilts his head to the side, watching me. I feel like I'm being examined under a magnifying glass. I have to look away.

"I think he might feel the same way." I barely hear myself speak.

The crinkle in Noah's forehead tells me he's thinking about something. I can only hope he's coming up with a solution for this spectacular mess.

"I can't see how any of this is bad," he says after a minute.

"You're joking, right?" I ask.

"Not at all."

I draw in a breath, trying to hold it the way Amarleen has us do in class when she wants us to relax. It doesn't work. My mind is reeling, and I can't figure out what Noah doesn't understand. I focus my eyes on him.

"My time here ends very soon, and I'm letting him get attached to me. How is that not a mistake?"

Noah stretches his legs out in front of him, crossing them at his ankles. It must be nice to be so at ease in a crisis.

"He needs to fall for you and open his heart, so he can develop his energy enough in this life to get to The Life-After. You know that, and you know he'll die if you don't make that happen." He sounds very matter-of-fact. "You're doing exactly what you should be and letting your instincts guide you. Trust what you feel, instead of what you tell yourself is right and wrong when you overthink it later."

I let go of the pillow, my fingers balling into fists. None of this fits together.

"Let me go back now and send someone else," I say, my voice flat. "There's still time for him. It's not like he met someone he never should have and had his destiny changed, like I did. You can figure something out." I can't do this to Riley, no matter what Noah believes the outcome will be.

"It's not as easy as you think it is. You were always part of the plan for Riley, and you leaving without helping him will change his destiny. And what about you and getting back to the Life-After? You know you can't go back until you're done here. Your energy isn't ready yet."

I try to focus on digging my fingernails into my palms, instead of on what I want to say to Noah right now. My self-restraint doesn't seem to matter, though, because he's reading every one of my thoughts.

"Frustration is an emotion that only exists here in The Before," he reminds me. "I know you've been here for a long time, but remember your energy is higher than that. You don't need to give in to it."

"You're not leaving me a whole lot of choices," I tell him. "I need your help, not a lecture."

"No." He shakes his head.

"Is that 'no' as in you won't help me?"

"It's no, you need to start helping yourself and rise above this. If you stay attached to the lower energy, you'll just fuel it with more energy and keep going down."

"That's encouraging." I set the throw pillow down beside me.

"It was supposed to snap you out of this," he replies.

I bite back the words I want to say, my hands twisting together in my lap while I try to think of how I can make him understand. Nothing comes to mind.

"I can't do this, and I don't believe that me leaving now will change Riley's destiny, at least not in a way you can't fix. I know you can fix it. Just please let me go back."

I can feel Noah's eyes on me, even though mine are focused firmly on the floor.

"You'll be back in a few weeks," he says. "This is what you're here for."

"To sit on my sofa, arguing with you?"

"To help Riley." I guess he's done with trying to scold me.

I flop back against the sofa cushions. "How am I supposed to help anyone when I'm a complete wreck?"

"You know you can't go back without finishing your work here." His voice is quiet, but it's also stern. "You need to learn how to control your energy and get it back up when you feel it sinking. Focus on this and you'll succeed at what you came here to do."

I shake my head, wondering why he can't just accept that what I'm telling him is the truth. If I could do what he's telling me to do, we wouldn't be having this conversation.

"This is different," I say. "The energy is stronger than me."

"It's not different. You've just never had a deep energy connection with anyone during your time back here, because you've refused to make friends or become close to other people. That would have helped."

I definitely don't want to go here. We've been arguing about this for years. I rub the bridge of my nose.

"That's not true. I was close to Selena."

"Uh-huh, and we both know what happened there. You pushed her away the first chance you had."

"I was protecting her. Why would I let someone get close to me when I knew I was leaving and that they wouldn't understand what dying really is?"

"You weren't protecting her. You were protecting yourself."

I could recite the rest of this argument word-for-word. Both of us know it's pointless. He doesn't get it and he never will. Of course, he thinks the same thing of me. I don't even have to hear his thoughts to know that. Time to skip to the part where we always end this.

"Let's say you're right, even though you're not," I say. "What am I supposed to do about it now? Go out and get some instant friends?"

"It's a little late now for easing into it."

"That's helpful." I let my head settle against the back of the sofa.

"You're just going to have to stay in tune with yourself. I need you to recognize when your energy is being lowered so you can separate yourself from it and raise it back up before you get like this." I don't answer, and he speaks again. "Starting now."

As if it's that easy. I'm sure my doubt is etched all over my face.

I hear him get to his feet and a moment later he sits down beside me on the sofa. "Take my hand," he says, his hand coming to rest on top of mine.

I do as I'm told, too tired to ask why. He grasps my hand between both of his and a feeling of calm surges through me.

"Close your eyes and focus," he tells me.

Even behind my closed eyes, I can see the sparks of golden light being infused into my energy. It goes on for what seems like hours, even though it's probably only a few minutes. When the light fades away, I sit with my eyes still closed until I hear Noah's voice.

"Welcome to your first energy transfusion. How do you feel?"

I blink a few times, letting the room come into focus. The edges of my mind feel fuzzy, but I'm calm. I wouldn't say I'm happy, exactly, but I feel better than I did before.

I shift my eyes over to him and have to blink again. Something doesn't look right. It's almost as if there's a haze around him. Blinking doesn't clear it, though, and after a moment I realize it's his energy. It's weaker, the glow more faint than I've ever seen it. He must have given me a lot.

"Are you okay?" I ask.

He nods, but I can tell how hard it is for him to do it. "I'll be fine. I just need to get back for a while."

He's drained, and it's because of me. "I'm sorry."

"Don't be sorry. Just promise me you'll try to keep your energy level strong. You don't have much longer to go." He picks up his fedora from the table and I sense it takes a lot of effort to do. Just something else to feel guilty for, I guess.

"I will." I don't really believe what I'm promising, but I don't know what else to say.

"Okay." Noah dons his hat, smiling at me. His face is tired. A second later, he's gone.

25

CHAPTER 25

"Hey, come sit with us." Lauren, my yoga classmate, pats the floor beside her mat.

It takes me a second or two to realize she's talking to me. I wave at her from inside the doorway, then head in her direction. I've been sitting close to Lauren and a few other people who are usually in this spot for a couple of weeks, even talking to them sometimes, but this is the first time anyone has invited me to sit with them.

"Thanks," I say, rolling out my mat on the floor beside her. When I turn around to put my purse behind me, I see Selena sitting in the corner of the room, watching me. She turns her head away when I look in her direction.

I'm sure she must take classes if she works here, I've just never seen her in Amarleen's class before. She's usually working at the front desk. Her words from our conversation in the bathroom spring into my mind. If you hurt Riley even a little bit, you won't be coming back here. I wonder if she's talked to Riley since then and knows that he took me to see John's band. Maybe she's here to keep an eye on me.

"You're just in time," Lauren sings from beside me. The glee in her voice is enough to distract me from Selena.

"In time for what?" I ask, bringing my legs out in front of me. I lean over and grab hold of my toes with my hands, trying to bring my nose down to touch my knees. Not quite. I'm halfway there, though, and that's progress from a couple of weeks ago.

"We're making plans for the yoga retreat. You should come with us."

"Retreat?" I echo. "I haven't heard about it."

"You'll love it." Lauren's face lights up. "It's the most fun weekend of the year. You should definitely come if you can."

"When is it?" I ask.

"It's not for another four weeks, but you get the discounted rate if you sign up now."

Four weeks. I won't be here then. I try to keep a smile on my face while I wrack my brain for something to say, since it sure can't be the truth.

"I think I'm going to be out of town. I'll let you know if that changes, though." It's not really a lie. Out of town means I won't be here, in L.A. The Life-After counts.

The classroom gets quiet then. I turn my head to the stage to see Amarleen bringing the microphone closer to her.

She smiles at all of us. "Sat Nam. Good morning." We return her greeting, sitting still on our mats.

She reaches for a piece of note paper that's in front of her on the stage and reads it silently. Then she looks out over the class. I follow her eyes and see them land on a girl who sits on the opposite side of the room from where I sit with Lauren. I hadn't noticed her until now. I would have, if I'd been paying attention to the energy in the room when I walked in. The girl's energy is weak, and I can see that it's the color of grief. Her face is etched with sadness.

"A man close to someone in this room passed away just a couple of nights ago," Amarleen says, still looking at the girl. "When a soul leaves their body, we often chant the word 'Akal' three times. It's a way for us to help send the soul home and help them transition to what's next." She turns her head to look at the rest of us in the room, her eyes stopping for a moment to hold mine. "Can we do that?"

I nod, watching most of the people around me do the same. The room fills with the sound of our voices, echoing from floor to ceiling and bouncing across the walls. The girl's eyes fill with tears when we've finished. She reaches for a tissue and uses it to wipe a teardrop that rolls down her cheek.

I want to tell her that the man she cares about is fine and that his life hasn't ended, but only just begun. If I could, I'd tell her that I'll be joining him soon, but she can talk to him any time she wants to and he'll hear her. That he knows she's here, and he knows we're sending him blessings. Most of all, I want to tell her that he's happier now than he ever was in The Before, because that's just the way it works in The Life-After.

I can't, though. So I connect my energy to hers for just a few moments instead, hoping it will strengthen her energy and help her heal. Amarleen turns her head to me just before I pull my energy back, giving me a small nod.

"Come talk to me after class?" she says, keeping her eyes on me. I nod. She turns back to the microphone and explains the first warm-up exercise. When I move to lie down on my back, I see Selena watching me again.

Selena leaves in a hurry once class is over. She doesn't look at me when she brushes by, instead keeping her eyes fixed on a spot in front of her. I linger, waiting for everyone else to leave the room so I can talk to Amarleen. Lauren rolls up her mat, touching my arm as she stands up.

"A few of us are going to have brunch outside on the patio, if you can stay."

I see Amarleen watching us. I nod at Lauren. "I'll be out in a few minutes."

She smiles and heads for the exit. Once she's through the doorway, I stand up and walk over to the stage. This is probably about the energy I sent out at the beginning of class. I can't tell if Amarleen approves of what I did, or if I'm in trouble.

"Can you close the door?" Amarleen asks.

I nod, backtracking to the door. I close it and then turn around again, making my way back to the stage.

"Come sit by me," she says. I do as she asks.

"You're doing really well, you know," she begins.

"Thank you," I say. I can't say I'm as confident about that as she is.

"It looks like you've found some friends here in class," she continues.

"Kind of, I guess." I'm not sure if I can call a few conversations and an invitation to a yoga retreat an actual friendship. It might be the beginnings of one, but it won't get very far and that's good. Lauren won't be hurt when I'm gone.

"Enjoy your friends here," she tells me. I start to speak again, but she's not finished. "I really mean that. Enjoy them, and enjoy your time with them. Don't be afraid of getting close. They can handle it, even if you don't think they can."

I blink hard. I realize then that she knows I'm leaving here soon. That shouldn't surprise me, I guess.

"The young man, too," she says. "Don't be afraid of getting close to him, either."

"The young man?" I repeat.

"You call him Riley when you think about him. Which is a lot, by the way."

I don't have anything to say to that, because I know it's true. I look down at my legs.

"You keep yourself pretty distant from most people, don't you?" she continues. I know it's an observation, not a question. She's been paying attention. I clear my throat. She waits for me to find my voice.

"I—I can't let people get close to me," I stutter. "It's not good for them." I hope she won't ask me why, although I sense she already knows.

"Or you can't let yourself get close to them." Her voice is gentle.

"Have you been talking to Noah?" I ask. That sure sounds like something that would come from him.

"No, I've just been watching you. I can tell you're afraid of what getting close to someone will do to you. Like with Selena."

My head snaps up.

26

CHAPTER 26

Either Amarleen saw how Selena was looking at me in class, or she remembers that we were avoiding each other at the front desk. Maybe both. I don't see how she could be getting this from just those two things, though. Not unless she overheard our conversation in the bathroom the other week. Now I'm positive that Noah said something to her.

"Noah didn't tell me anything," she says, reading my thoughts. "I've seen the energy between you and Selena. It tells me you were close once, and for a long time. You had a falling out, I'm guessing?"

"Sort of." I pause, wondering if there's an easy way to explain this. Then I remember that she can hear my thoughts, which makes me wonder if she can also see my memories if she tunes into my energy. Noah can. I look up at her, and she gives me an encouraging smile. I think she already knows what I'm going to ask her.

"Can I show you, if I think of the memory that I have?"

She nods. "I should be able to see it. Just close your eyes and relax, and picture what you want me to see."

I close my eyes and breathe slowly and deeply. When my mind is completely still, I let an image of myself as a little girl surface. It's faint at first, then it gets stronger until I'm right there in the memory, watching it all unfold in front of me.

I'm sitting on a swing set in my aunt and uncle's backyard, the new metal poles a sparkly pink that I love. Someone came to set it up yesterday, and it's only the second time I've sat on one of the white plastic seats. I'm six years old and I haven't been living with my aunt and uncle for very long.

My uncle stands behind me, making sure I'm steady on the seat and that I won't fall off. He doesn't know that no harm would come to me even if I did take a tumble, but it's a secret I have to keep for my own. My aunt was outside with us until a couple of minutes ago, but she went inside when our housekeeper came to tell her there was someone at the door.

I try to push myself on the swing with my legs. The swing is a little too high, though. My toes barely touch the ground.

"Need some help?" my uncle asks. I nod. He takes the chains of the swing in his hand and gives me a small push, just enough to help me rock back and forth but not enough to send me sailing through the air. I'm about to ask him to push the swing harder when my aunt appears in the doorway that opens out to the backyard.

My aunt isn't alone. There's a woman standing beside her. She holds the hand of a girl who looks to be about my age. The girl stares at me from the doorway until the woman kneels down and says something to her, and then gestures to me.

The girl's eyes light up, and then she races across the lawn toward me. She's at my side within seconds, hopping onto the swing beside me.

"I'm Selena," she says, taking hold of the chains on either side of her swing. She's a little bit taller than me and uses her feet to start pushing herself.

"I'm Cassidy," I tell her. My swing isn't going anywhere so I watch her swing back and forth, her dark curls bouncing around her face.

"Selena, don't forget what we brought with us," the woman calls from across the yard.

Selena hops off the swing and goes scampering back over to her. The woman hands her a rectangular package wrapped in rainbow foil and a ton of curled ribbons. I get off of the swing and take a few steps toward them. Selena rushes to meet me, her eyes sparkling and her face eager as I open the gift. It's a princess doll.

"I have one too," Selena says. "It's my favorite. We can play with them together and pretend they're twin sisters."

And that's exactly what we did. I fast forward in time, another memory surfacing from my first day at my new school. Selena and I sit at desks beside each other, something we did whenever we could until we were assigned to different classes in junior high.

More pictures of Selena and me together flash through my mind, stopping when we're in the tenth grade. Selena's in my bedroom, tears streaming down her face. I hug her, asking what's wrong, but she starts to sputter and choke every time she speaks. I keep hugging her until she calms down enough for her sobs to become sniffles.

"We're moving in a month," she finally says, wiping the tears from her cheeks with her sleeve. "We're not going to live in Boston anymore." It takes me the better part of an hour to get the whole story. Her father is going to head up his law firm's new office in L.A., and her parents are taking her away from me. To hear her tell it, they're absolutely ruining her life.

Selena sleeps over at my house every night that week, refusing to be separated from me for a second longer than she has to be. Finally, her parents make her come home. When I'm alone again, for the first time in days, it hits me how distraught Selena is about moving thousands of miles away. It's only distance, I know, but she doesn't see it like that. If she's this upset about moving to another city, I don't want to think about what she'll be like if we're still close friends when I leave for The Life-After in a couple of years.

It takes a few days, but I make the decision I know I must. On the night of her family's going-away party, I do what I have to do. I let Amarleen see the party and the conversation in the garden. I let her see me walking away, and I let her see the tears I don't show Selena or anyone else. Then I let the memories fade.

It's the touch of Amarleen's hand on my shoulder that makes me open my eyes.

"I understand," she tells me, her voice softer than usual. She keeps her eyes on me. I can tell there's something else she wants to say.

"But?" I prompt her.

"But it's time to let go and let yourself be open. You keep yourself from seeing that. The past is a tricky thing and we let it define us when we should embrace the here and now, and all that's still coming. You need to let yourself live from a place of love, not from a place of fear over the things you can't control."

That all sounds good. Well, in theory. But it doesn't tell me what to do when it's the thought of hurting someone I love that makes me afraid.

Amarleen studies me. I know she heard that.

"I know you think your fears and what you're doing come from a place of love. Just remember that true love comes from love only, and it isn't based in fear. You'll know what to do when it's time if you can rise above the fear and let love win." I'm about to protest, but she stops me. "Trust in yourself, trust in the energy you've been working on, and trust what your heart and the voice inside of you tell you to do. And most importantly, don't let a downward spiral of energy influence what you do, or what you decide. Otherwise, it might not be your inner guidance helping you make your decision at all."

I feel warmth wash over me and know she's connecting her energy with mine. We sit there for a minute or two and I can feel my energy get stronger, little white and golden sparks dancing around me.

"Now if I'm not mistaken, I think you have some people waiting for you on the patio? You should go join your friends."

My friends. Maybe it's the strength of her energy connected with mine, but the thought makes me smile as I collect my yoga mat and head for the door.

27

— • —

CHAPTER 27

Countdown to The Life-After: two weeks.

I was a morning person for most of my life as Anna, rising early to jog along the beach and watching golden light streak the sky as the sun came up. I loved the peace in the space between darkness and dawn, and weekend mornings were my favorite.

Even now when I wake up early enough on a weekend day, the world feels like my own. There's a stillness in the morning that holds an entirely different kind of energy than is usually found here in The Before. I felt it during my time here as Anna, even though I knew nothing about energy then.

The early hours cleanse me somehow. I jog along the sand, listening to the ocean waves crash to the shore and taking in every detail. This is the beach I'll come to on the morning I leave for The Life-After. Sunlight licks at the edges of the sky. I breathe in the salty air that's already warming in the daylight.

I jog for about a mile before I see a figure far off down the beach, moving closer toward me. Even from this distance, and even with sunglasses shielding his eyes, I recognize him.

"Riley?" I call out.

He looks up and I can tell I've startled him. When he sees me, he slows to a walk and raises his arm, waving once.

"Hey," I say, when I get closer.

"Hi," he answers. I expect a hug, but he puts his hands on his hips and turns his head to the ocean. There's a look on his face I can't quite figure out. He's probably thinking about The Satellite, since we haven't hung out since then. It's been a week. I know that's what I'm thinking about.

"I didn't know you came out here to run," I say. He turns his head back to me.

"I usually don't." The look on his face is still there.

"It's a nice place for it," I comment. He nods. I wish I could see his eyes, but they're hidden behind his sunglasses.

I take a drink from my water bottle, not knowing what else to do. After swallowing my mouthful of water, I study him. His lips are pressed together and his jaw looks like it's clenched. I tune in to his energy to see what else I can find. The sparks of color I see are about what I expected. He's uncomfortable and maybe even a little anxious. I guess I have my brilliant comment about him kissing me one day to thank for that. Genius. He probably regrets repeating it back to me. I did this, and now I have to undo it.

"Want to run with me?" I ask.

"Yeah, sure." His arms still look a little stiff at his sides.

"Is everything okay?" The question slips out of my mouth even though I probably shouldn't ask.

"Yeah," he says again, and tries to smile at me. "Sorry. I wasn't expecting to see you here."

I give him a small smile in return and start jogging in the direction he came from. He keeps pace at my side, both of us moving in silence for about half a mile.

"Did you have a good time the other night?"

I jump at the sound of his voice, stumbling over my feet. Nothing but grace over here. Riley's hand shoots out to steady me and we both slow down a little.

"I didn't mean to startle you."

I wave it off, even though that's exactly what happened. "I was just off on another planet somewhere." A planet decorated like it's space alien Christmas in 1972. It counts.

We round the side of a cliff. I can't see the part of the beach we came from anymore. This is like some private little cove. Riley slows to a walk and I do, too. I can tell he's still waiting for an answer.

"I had a great time," I finally say. It's the truth, because I really did have a great time. If only the part of my brain that controls my mouth hadn't decided it was a good time to go rogue. Minor technicality.

"I'm glad. John said they have another show coming up in a few weeks, if you want to go."

A few weeks. As much as I want to yell out that yes, I want to go, I know I won't be here when the show happens. Whether I'll be in The Life-After or just gone to wherever it is unsuccessful second-timers go is another story.

"I'd love to go," I hear myself say. I even smile. Way to lie to him.

We're almost shoulder-to-shoulder now, so close that his arm bumps against mine when he crouches down to pick up a conch shell from the beach. He holds it up to his ear.

"Can you hear the ocean in it?" I ask.

He moves the shell away from his ear and presses it against mine. I listen to the sound inside of the shell, my other ear still picking up the sound of the ocean waves beside us.

"That's amazing." I turn to him and see he's staring at me with the same intensity he did outside of his car at The Satellite. My eyes drop to the sand. I wonder if he can hear my heart pounding, because right now that's the only sound filling my ears.

He lowers the shell from my ear and places it in my hand.

"It's all yours."

My fingers brush against his when he moves his hand away and I feel the tingle that tells me our energy is connected again.

We walk for a few more minutes. I wonder if I should reach for his hand and then wonder if I'm crazy for thinking that. I try to keep my eyes focused on the beach ahead of us instead of on him, and a flash of pink ahead provides a welcome distraction. I crane my neck to see what it is. It looks like a bouquet of pink roses.

"Did someone leave flowers on the beach?" I ask.

Riley doesn't answer. I'm a few paces ahead of him when I realize he's come to a complete stop.

"Do you want to go—" I start, cutting off my words when I see his face. There's that strange look again, like he had when I first saw him walking toward me on the beach. "Is something wrong?"

He doesn't answer. I follow his eyes with mine and see him looking at the flowers.

Wait. It's Noah's voice I hear.

I wait like he tells me, and it takes only a couple of seconds before everything in front of me blurs. When my surroundings come into focus again, the bouquet is no longer where it was. I see Riley approaching from far off down the beach, carrying the bouquet in his arms. He stops when he gets to the spot where the flowers were when I noticed them, and kneels down in the sand. He sets the bouquet down, his head bent forward, and I see something I've only seen on his face in another vision. Anguish. He remains there, motionless. What I'm watching fades away and then I'm back where I was before, Riley still standing beside me and the flowers still ahead of us on the beach. Now it makes sense.

"Did you bring the flowers here?" I ask.

He doesn't answer, just closes his eyes, and I feel his energy retreating. I know who the flowers are for.

"Is this where your friend died?"

He turns to face the ocean, leaving me staring at his back. "I don't want to talk about it."

"She's here with you, you know. You just don't feel her."

"She's dead." There's an edge in his voice that's warning me to back off, but I don't.

"Do you think this body is all we are, and that this is all there is?"

He turns back around to face me. I spread my arms out wide, trying to ignore the way he's looking at me like I'm crazy.

"This is all I can see, hear, touch, feel, and smell. So yes, I think this is where it all ends." His voice is flat.

You can see, hear, touch, feel, and smell me, I want to shout at him. I don't.

"You have to stop and let go," I say instead. It's almost laughable that this advice is coming from me, but I paid a big price for what I know now. It's my job to make sure he doesn't make the same mistake I did, and get so caught up in grief that the lower energy overpowers him and eats at him until he's left with a dead spot just like mine. If that happens, this life is done for him and he'll have to come back here.

And if that happens, I'll never see this place or The Life-After again.

"If I could, don't you think I would?" There's a waver in his voice. I know I should take that as my cue to stop. My mouth seems to be under the control of something other than logic, though.

"I don't think you're trying."

He rubs the side of his face. "Like you would know."

"I know a lot more than you think." I don't mean for him to hear me, but I may as well have hollered the words. He looks up like someone slapped him.

"You were six when your parents died. Not to take anything away from that, but how much can you really remember? Try losing someone you love when you're eighteen, like you are right now. There's no way you can understand what this is like."

I want to tell him that I didn't mean my parents, and that I know all too well what he's going through. He's handling it better than I did, though, because how I dealt with it cost me my life and robbed me of at least eighteen years in The Life-After. Eighteen years that I should have spent feeling happy and being surrounded by love.

He sits down on the sand, his hands coming to rest on his knees. I sit down beside him.

"You can talk to me, you know. Talking about your friend and what you're feeling might be good for you, and I'd like to know more about her. I can tell she meant a lot to you."

"You don't need to know everything, you know. It's not like you're my girlfrie—" he stops. It's too late, though. The words are out there now, hanging in the air.

"It's not like I'm your girlfriend," I finish for him.

"That's not what I meant."

"Maybe not, but it's true. Right?" I realize I'm biting my lip and stop before I draw blood.

He focuses his eyes on me. "That came out wrong."

"It's fine." I stare out at the ocean. "You're right that I don't need to know everything. I'm not your girlfriend, and you're not my boyfriend, and we're not dating. I think that covers it."

"I never said we're not dating."

I look at him. "No, I did." I try not to wince. Now that the words are out of my mouth, I know I can't take them back.

He doesn't respond, just takes a deep breath and releases it, raking a hand through his hair.

"I need to go," he says. I watch him get to his feet.

"So go."

He hesitates, either because he wants to say something or because he wants me to. I turn my head back to the ocean and pretend to watch the waves until I hear the soft thud of his footsteps on the sand, walking away.

It's good that he isn't attached to me, I try to tell myself. No matter what Noah says, it's better this way. I just didn't expect knowing that to hurt this much.

28

CHAPTER 28

I holler out the chorus of a song I must have played at least ten times already today, stirring the boiling water in a pot on the stove. If I lose my voice later, that's fine. It only gets me into trouble, anyway.

If I were my own neighbor, I'm sure I'd hate myself right now. I've had music cranked for most of the day, the bass thumping so loudly that it vibrates the pictures on the walls and my kitchen windows. I can't hear myself think, and that's entirely the point.

"Do you want to talk about it?"

I jump. My hand that's holding a wooden spoon and stirring a steaming pot of macaroni comes up with me, spraying water droplets all over my arm. I suck in my breath at what feels like dozens of tiny needles burning into my skin. It figures I'd scald myself while making mac and cheese. It was supposed to be comfort food.

"As always, your timing is fantastic." I wave the spoon at Noah before setting it down on the counter and crossing my arms. "Was that really necessary?"

"To be here? Absolutely." He reaches for the volume knob on the stereo and turns it down.

"To maim me," I correct him.

"I think you'll make it until all of your pain goes away in The Life-After." I do a double take. Sarcasm is my thing, not his.

"Touché. What is it you think I want to talk about?"

"I'm pretty sure you know." He takes off his fedora.

I turn back to the stove. "I love you, but you aren't helping me much."

"Someone else loves you, too, but I think you know that."

"That's doubtful, if we're thinking of the same person. You were watching us at the beach this morning, unless you stopped right after that little vision of Riley leaving the flowers." I pick up the spoon from the counter and stir the macaroni again.

"I saw everything, and don't try to act like you weren't a good part of that. People say things they don't mean to when they're provoked, and I think you provoked him on purpose."

I stop stirring, my hand tightening around the wooden spoon. "Do you want to repeat that one?"

"Sure." He leans against the counter, looking at me. I move my eyes back to the pot of boiling water. "I think you wanted that fight today, but there's one thing I can't figure out."

I start stirring again. "What's that?"

"Are you afraid of what happens when you leave him, or are you afraid of him leaving you?"

"You're really asking me this? Ow!" Water spits out of the pot and onto my arm. I grit my teeth, grabbing onto my hand.

"Turn down the heat on that." Noah reaches over and adjusts the heat dial for the element. The water in the pot slows to a gentle boil. "And yes, I'm really asking you that."

"Why?"

"Because I think it's a question you need to answer for yourself, and I hope you'll be honest about it."

I give the macaroni another stir. "Why is it you think you know so much?"

I feel Noah's energy connecting with mine. He's trying to calm me down. Good luck, buddy.

"Because I know a bit about what goes on in your head and heart," he answers. "I'm not trying to be cruel."

"So why are you asking me to think about this?"

"You need to. You'll feel better when you do. There's almost no point to you being here if you're going to keep putting blocks in your own way just because you're afraid." The guy is a broken record, I swear.

"I thought I was here to help Riley," I say.

"You can't be much help to him when you're barely stumbling through your own life here." He leans back against the counter, watching me.

"I'm trying. Riley's not the greatest at opening up, if you haven't noticed. He starts to and then he backs away."

"And you?"

"And me?" I ask. "I don't follow."

"In those moments after you open up, do you also take a step back?"

"I don't think so." I put the wooden spoon down on the counter.

"Uh huh. Did he push away this time, or did you?"

"You were there," I tell him.

"I want your take on this."

"Maybe we both did," I say quietly.

"At least one of you shouldn't have. You're the one who knows better, since you have a job to do. What you saw on the beach should have made you more sensitive to that. You're supposed to help him get past his pain, not close off when he reacts to it. Of anyone, you know what he's going through."

"Sure, kick me when I'm down." I walk over to the stereo and crank the volume back up, then go back to the stove.

"Stop acting like you're six, and start acting like a second-timer." He turns the volume back down.

"You can turn that back up if you're going to keep lecturing me."

He ignores me. "I want you to go find him."

"I'll text him," I mumble.

"I didn't say text him. I said go find him."

"And what do I say when I get there?" I pick up the spoon and give the macaroni one last stir, and then turn off the element.

"You could start with hello."

"Sheer brilliance. Do you write scripts in your spare time?"

He doesn't answer me. I open the cupboard beside the stove and grab a colander from one of the shelves. I bring it over to the sink and pour the contents of the pot into it, letting the water drain out.

"What do I say?" I ask again, watching the water go down the drain. Steam rises from the sink.

"You'll know what to say. Just listen to your heart instead of your fear."

Amarleen said the same thing. I open my mouth to ask him if he's getting his lines from her, but he's gone.

"Thanks for leaving me on my own for this one," I call out. I think I hear a chuckle somewhere in the distance.

29

CHAPTER 29

My footsteps echo on the stairs leading up to Riley's apartment, so loudly he can probably hear me coming from inside. When I have to pause to cough, I realize that my mouth and throat have both gone dry. That's funny, because my palms are damp. I swallow, trying to moisten my throat so I don't cough again, and then take the last two steps while trying to remember to breathe.

Shoulders back, head and chin up, I command myself. I raise my hand and my knuckles meet the cool surface of the door. After three short but loud raps, I lower my hand and wait.

About thirty seconds pass before I try knocking again, but there's still no answer. I can't hear any noises coming from inside.

Brilliant, Noah, I think. You insist—no, command—that I come over here, and he's not even home. You didn't see that one coming?

Noah doesn't answer me, though, and I know that I'm on my own. I turn around and head down the stairs, intending to go back to my car. Riley's mom is standing in front of the studio when I round the corner, though, and I stop in my tracks when she turns her head to look at me.

"Hi, Cassidy. Are you looking for Riley?" She seems happy to see me, I notice. I guess Riley hasn't mentioned anything about our morning at the beach.

"Hi, Mrs. Da— Elizabeth. Yeah, I thought he might be here." I hear gravel crunching below my feet and realize I'm shifting from foot to foot. I force myself to stand still.

She shakes her head. "He left a while ago to go write. He said he needed a change of scenery to focus and clear his head."

Awesome. I'm probably the one to blame for that. "Do you know where he is?" I ask, trying to sound casual.

"He went to a coffee shop that's a few blocks from here. Malone's, I think it's called. It's somewhere near the Promenade, if you want to go say hi."

I get the sense that she's asking me to go find him, even though I'll be interrupting his writing time. I wonder how much she's worried about him since Amanda left this life.

"Thanks. I'll, uh, go see if I can find him." I start walking again.

"Cassidy?" I turn back to her. "It's good to see you."

There's genuine warmth in her smile. It makes me wish I had enough time left here to get to know her.

"It's good to see you, too."

She opens the door to the studio and goes inside, and I keep walking to my car. When I'm inside of it, I pull my phone out of my purse and search for the coffee shop she mentioned. It takes only a minute or two to find it and pull up driving directions. I just have to hope that Riley is still there.

The street the coffee shop is on is close by. It's only a few minutes before I pull into a parking garage that's on the same street and then head out to the sidewalk.

Here we go, all over again. I put one foot in front of the other, trying to think of what I'll say when I see him.

And there he is, sitting inside of the coffee shop, scribbling on a notepad. As I look through the coffee shop window, I see him pause to take a sip from his mug before bringing the pen back to the page. Another minute passes by while I watch him write, my feet rooted to the sidewalk.

I can do this, I think. Gulping in a lungful of air, I force my feet forward again. Chimes tinkle above the door when I push it open.

"Hi there," the barista calls out from behind the counter. He gives me a quick wave and then returns to flipping through a magazine.

Riley looks up at the doorway. Our eyes lock and neither of us moves for a few moments, until he sets his pen down on the table. It rolls away and clatters onto the floor, but he makes no move to pick it up. I can't even be sure he's blinking, or that I am either.

I raise my hand and wiggle my fingers in something that I hope resembles a wave, but he still sits there, motionless. He's not looking away from me or bolting, though, so that's a good sign. Or at least I think it is, and that's all I have to go on right now.

He looks like a deer caught in the headlights, and I'm sure I do, too. The thought causes my lips to curve up in a smile, and I curse the bad timing. Maybe not, though, because is that the barest of smiles on his face, too? That's a million times better than a scowl or frown, anyway. Time to take the next step.

I adjust the shoulder strap of my purse and take a step toward him. He sits up straight in his chair but says nothing. It appears that the writer is at a loss for words.

"Is this chair free?" I ask, placing my hand on the back of the wooden chair beside him.

He swallows and clears his throat. "Ah, yeah. There's no one at this table but me."

I smile again and sit down, trying to ignore the flutter in my stomach and how nervous I am now that I'm here. No, make that terrified.

"What are you working on?" I ask him, looking down at the pages filled with his hastily-scrawled words. I see arrows in some places connecting sentences together, and bubbles of point-form notes in others, all mixed in with the paragraphs that fill each page.

"A novel I'm writing." He's staring at me and then seems to realize it. Shifting his eyes away, he reaches for his mug and takes a drink from it.

"Can I read it sometime?" I ask. I won't be here in The Before when he's finished writing it, I know, but I'll find a way to read it from The Life-After.

"Maybe when it's a little more polished. It's a little hard to follow like this." He puts his mug down. I watch him, silent, until he speaks again. "Why are you here?"

"I have this thing with lost causes." His eyes widen and I review my words in my head. Yeah, that definitely didn't come out the way I meant it. "You're not the lost cause," I rush to add.

He grins. "I could argue that."

"Of the two of us, I think I'm the lost cause here." I feel myself starting to relax.

"No, you're not. And maybe..." he pauses, swallowing again. "Maybe we're not, either," he finishes. He reaches across the table to touch my hand and I realize that as much as my being here has caught him by surprise, he's glad I came.

I flip my hand under his so we're palm to palm. Maybe there are things he can't say, but I can feel them in his touch and see them in his energy. It's expanding now, reaching out toward me.

"Maybe we're not," I agree, my voice soft. My body tingles as our energy connects. Even though he probably can't feel it, I can tell it's affecting him, too. I see it in the way he watches me, and how his breath catches and gets a little shallower. He looks down at our hands, tracing a pattern on my palm. He keeps his eyes there long enough for me to wonder if he's having trouble looking at me.

Now is not the time to be shy, I think. He looks up again like he heard me, holding my eyes with his.

"Do you want to go for a walk?" he asks.

30

CHAPTER 30

I can hear what Riley isn't saying. He wants to go somewhere that isn't lit up with harsh fluorescent lights, and where our words won't bounce around the room for the barista or anyone else to hear.

"Yes."

He squeezes my fingers again and then lets go of them to lean over and scoop up his pen from the floor. He slips it inside of the messenger bag that hangs on the side of his chair. He does the same with the papers he gathers up from the table. "Okay, senorita. Let's jet."

I push my chair back from the table. The scraping noise makes the barista look up from his magazine.

"Thank you," he calls out.

Riley raises his hand to wave goodbye. As he lowers it, he reaches out to take my hand again, sending another tingle of energy through me. Our fingers stay joined together as we leave the café and step out into the evening air.

I let him lead, watching the energy surrounding him from the corner of my eye. Even if I wasn't able to see the sparks dancing around him, I would be able to feel them from the touch of his hand on mine. The color of his energy tells me he's nervous.

"What are you thinking about?" he asks. We get to an intersection and stop walking, waiting for the red light in front of us to turn green.

"You," I answer.

"Only good things, I hope. Not that I think I deserve that." His hold on my hand gets a little bit tighter, enough to let me feel how fast his pulse is racing. It matches mine.

"I think we're both to blame for this morning."

His free arm circles around me, nudging me closer. I let him pull me into a hug, my head buried in his chest. His chin comes to rest on top of my head.

"How did you know I wanted to see you tonight?" he murmurs. He keeps his arm around me. I realize then that I don't ever want him to let go.

"Something guided me here," I say, silently thanking Noah for the very thing I wanted to throttle him for earlier tonight.

"I can be kind of a jerk sometimes, I know. I'm sorry."

"Don't apologize." I move my head so I can look at him.

"I don't know why I do it," he continues. "I mean, I know why I do it. But I shouldn't do it." The nervousness that I saw in his energy seeps into his voice.

I squeeze his hand, bringing my free hand up to touch the side of his cheek. I don't say a word, because I know I don't have to. He turns his head to kiss the palm of my hand, his eyes still locked on mine.

My hand moves up to brush against the side of his hair and then he's lowering his head, his face close to mine like it's been before. This time, though, he keeps getting closer, until there's no space between us and his lips are touching mine. His kiss is feather light at first, like he's not sure how I'll respond. I bring my other hand up to join the one that's now tangling through his hair, and I feel his arms tighten around me. I've kissed someone before, in another body and another life, but I don't remember it feeling like this. The sparks of energy between us pop like little firecrackers, making me tingle from head to toe.

He captures my bottom lip with both of his and then grazes it with his teeth, and suddenly what was so tentative at first is filled with the intensity of the weeks gone by. His tongue traces the inside of my lips before we break apart, and I keep my eyes closed when I feel the lightest trail of kisses along my jawbone and neck.

His lips press against my collarbone and his head comes to rest there. I circle my arms around his waist, holding him close. We stay like that for a couple of minutes, just standing in the middle of the sidewalk. I don't know if anyone is watching us, and I don't care if they are. If I could capture one moment of my life and hold onto it forever, this would be it.

I feel his arms loosen their hold around me and I look up at him. He looks a little bit shy now, taking my hand. We start walking again.

"Do you want to come over for a while?" His voice is a little husky and I think he realizes it, because he clears his throat. "Time for a Mario Kart rematch, so I can blow you away."

"The first time when I completely destroyed you was just a practice round, right?"

"Absolutely." He smiles, looking down at the ground first and then at me. There's that shyness again. We walk down the street for a few more blocks and then circle back until we're outside of the parking garage where my car is parked.

"I'm parked here," I tell him, pointing at the garage. "I'll meet you at your place?"

"I'll walk you to your car." He doesn't need to, but I can tell he wants to. That's more than okay with me, because I don't really want to let go of his hand just yet.

I lead him to the elevator on the first floor of the garage, both of us stepping inside when the doors open. I press the button for the top floor and the doors close again.

Sometimes elevators can be like little boxes of truth. Together in this tiny little space, I feel our energy heightened to a level even greater than it was out in the open. Leaning against Riley with my head on his shoulder, I feel everything inside of me tingle. He doesn't look shy now for some reason, and I can tell he wants to kiss me again just as much as I want to kiss him. We hold back, though, letting the beautiful buzz between us grow. Neither of us notices when the elevator comes to a stop and the doors open.

"Are you getting out here?" A man's voice draws my attention to the open door. He puts his arm against it to keep it from closing. I'm sure that on a normal night, I'd have some passing thought about patience and the guy's lack of it. Tonight I just nod and lead Riley out of the elevator into the parking garage. The man steps into the elevator and the doors close, leaving us alone again.

"I'm just over there," I tell Riley, tilting my head in the direction of my car. We walk the short distance together, and he drops a kiss on the top of my head before letting me get inside.

"See you in a few minutes?" he asks.

"Better get ready to be taken down at Mario Kart again." I hear him laugh before my door shuts. Once I have my seat belt on, he raises his hand and then turns to walk back to the elevator.

It takes only a few minutes to find my way to his place, driving back down the roads I took to get to the coffee shop. I park in the same spot on the street where I parked earlier tonight and wait inside of my car until I see headlights coming up the road behind me.

Riley doesn't say anything when he gets out of his car. He just holds my eyes with his. We walk around the back of the studio, our feet scuffling against the pavement.

He fumbles with his keys when we reach the top of the stairs, his keychain jangling in his hand until he finds the right one and slides it into the lock on the door. He turns the doorknob and pushes the door open, then squeezes my hand.

I walk inside ahead of him until I'm standing at the edge of the living room, not sure where to go or what to do. I hear the door shut and his footsteps on the floor, walking toward me. His hands touch my shoulders a second later. He must feel how tense they are, because he starts to massage them.

"Want to sit down?" He stops rubbing my shoulders, but keeps his hands there.

I bring my hands up to cover his. Instead of moving to the sofa, I find myself turning around to face him. Then his finger is below my chin, tilting my head up to his. Our lips meet and his body presses against mine, but it somehow doesn't feel like we could ever be close enough. His hands move to cradle my face, deepening the kiss. My hands snake up his back and we don't stop kissing until both of us need to catch our breath. When we break apart, he takes my hand and leads me over to the sofa, pulling me down beside him.

"I need to talk to you for a second." He looks sheepish, almost embarrassed. I think I nod, but I'm too caught up in thinking that whatever this is, anything that starts with I need to talk to you can't be good.

"You know how much I care about you, don't you?" he continues. Nope, this definitely isn't good. I don't say anything, though, and just nod again, not trusting my voice.

"Okay." He takes a breath. When I look down at his hand, I see that it's shaking. Definitely a bad sign. It takes me a second to realize he's talking again.

"If I tell you something, will you trust and know that it's coming from my heart and that it's not just the moment?"

"Sure," I manage to croak. I'm expecting the worst until I tune into his energy and see a pink and gold glow around him. It's then that I know to expect something else entirely.

"I didn't mean what I said earlier today, at the beach," he says.

"I know," I tell him. "I didn't mean what I said, either."

He cups my cheek in his palm and closes his eyes for a few seconds. When he opens them, he stares straight into my eyes.

"I haven't dated anyone since—" he stops, his eyes moving to the photograph of him and Amanda. I wait for him to take a breath. "Since Amanda died," he continues. "I didn't think I could. I don't even know if I can tell you what it was like when she was just gone."

I want to tell him that I know, and that it's okay, but something in his eyes makes me stop. He brings his hand down, letting it rest on my knee.

"You changed that, though, because I love you."

The tingle of energy running through me is more intense than anything I've ever felt. It's so strong that when I open my mouth, I find that I can't speak. In the momentary absence of words, I bring my hands to his face and gently press my lips to his forehead.

"I love you, too," I tell him, once I can form words again. I lower my hands, rubbing my thumbs along the backs of his fingers.

He pulls me closer, kissing the top of my head and then my eyebrow. I close my eyes before he kisses each eyelid, then feel him brush his lips against the tip of my nose. Unable to wait any longer, I move my head and capture his mouth with mine. His arms slide around my body. I feel myself easing backward, effortlessly, until I'm on my back against the sofa cushions and he's above me, his body pressed against mine. His lips move down to the hollow of my throat, my shoulder, and finally, my collarbone. He lingers there for a few seconds and then brings his mouth back up to find mine again.

For the first time since I left The Life-After, I think I know what it's like to be truly alive.

31

CHAPTER 31

I wake up to rays of sunshine pouring through Riley's bedroom window. We fell asleep here together last night, and I realize that I'm going to look like a complete mess when I get up. My clothes are wrinkled from sleeping in them and I know my slept-on hair is probably sticking out everywhere. It doesn't matter, though, because I'm here right now with Riley's arms around me, feeling his chest rise and fall with the even breath of sleep. I wonder if he'll keep his arms around me when he wakes up.

I move my head a little bit so I can see his face. He looks peaceful, his lips parted just slightly and his eyelashes resting against his cheeks. I tune in to his energy and see the same deep pink and golden sparks that I did last night. They're more brilliant now than they were then, which I hadn't thought possible.

He stirs and then his eyes open. A sleepy smile appears on his face when he sees me and he closes his eyes again, holding me a little tighter. He buries his head in the back of my hair and I feel the familiar tingle of our energy connecting. He's here to stay, I know, and I wish I was staying, too.

Don't think about that now, I tell myself. A soft kiss on my shoulder pulls me back into this moment, and I'm grateful.

"You look so serious. What are you thinking about?" His voice is still hoarse from sleep.

"Coffee," I murmur. He laughs, and the sound of it makes me feel warm everywhere. I shift my body so I'm facing him. "That can wait for a bit, though."

"You're sure about that? Coffee is pretty serious business." He brushes a strand of hair from my cheek.

"Shhh." I put a finger against his lips and he smiles, pulling me close again.

"I can't see the clock from here. Do you know what time it is?"

I raise my head to look at the clock on his bedside table. "Almost seven-thirty."

It's no wonder both of us are still sleepy, given that we fell asleep sometime after two o'clock in the morning. I settle my head against the pillow and notice his smile start to fade.

"Now you're the one who looks serious," I tell him. "What are you thinking about?"

"Work." He wrinkles his nose. "I'm supposed to be at the studio today. Do you think my mom will go for it if I call in sick?"

He pretends to cough. It's the worst fake cough I've ever heard. I giggle and shake my head.

"No, huh? There goes my acting career."

"Better stick to writing," I tease him, kissing his nose.

"How about this?" I feel his mouth tug on my lower lip. My hands make their way up his back until they're in his hair. He covers my mouth with his and I feel our bodies press closer, our legs tangling together.

"Mmm." He slowly moves his mouth away from mine. I can tell he doesn't want to.

"Definitely keep doing that," I manage to say, even though I'm so light-headed that I don't think I can move. "Please practice a lot."

"Oh yeah?" He bends his head over mine and kisses me again, this time until I really think the world is spinning. I feel his fingers play at the hem of my shirt, and then the warmth of his palm against my skin. His hand inches upward and his kiss gets hungrier. My breath catches when I feel his thumb stroke the curve of my chest and even though it probably isn't possible, I try to pull him closer against me. His mouth moves away from mine and when I feel his breath tickle my face, I realize it's because he's laughing.

"What's funny?" I open my eyes.

He shakes his head. "Not funny. Just amazing." His head dips down to kiss the side of my neck. His lips move to my earlobe, sending a flutter through my body.

"Do you have any idea what you're doing to me right now?" I murmur. He doesn't answer me with words, but releases my earlobe and brings his mouth to my eyebrow and then to the tip of my nose. I tilt my head up, trying to bring my lips to his. He hovers as close as he can without touching, mischief sparkling in his eyes.

"What do you want me to do to you right now?" he asks.

What a question. My mind takes off with about a million possibilities and my face must show it because Riley chuckles again, moving ever-so-slightly closer to touch his lips to mine. This kiss is gentle.

"It might be a good thing that I have to get up for work," he says when we break apart. "Keeps me responsible." I can tell from the face he makes that it's the last thing he wants to be, but he's right. I force my breath to slow down.

"Should I let you get ready?" I ask.

He squeezes my shoulder and nods. The look of little-boy regret on his face makes me giggle. I can tell he wants to continue where we just left off, but he forces himself to get out of bed.

He makes both of us scrambled eggs and toast before letting me leave. I feel like I'm floating on air after kissing him goodbye and walking to my car.

I get into the driver's seat and put the key in the ignition. Then I stop. I don't know why, but something makes me turn my head and look at the house across the street. Selena's house.

There's nobody standing in the driveway this time. I don't even see a car parked outside. The curtains on all of the windows are closed. There's no reason I should be watching the house. It's like I'm waiting for the front door to open and for Selena to appear. I should just turn the key, start my car, and go home.

But I can't. Maybe it's the sleep I didn't have last night, or some sort of energy hangover from the hours next to Riley. Maybe it's something else. The conversation I had with Amarleen plays in my mind while I watch the house. Live from a place of love.

I open the glove compartment and reach inside, pulling out the first piece of paper I see. The white feather I put in there weeks ago falls out and flutters to the floor of my car. I let it stay where it lands and dig through my purse until I find a pen. Then I hold the piece of paper against the car door window while I scribble the only words I can think to say.

Dear Selena,I'm sorry.- Cassidy

Five words. I don't know what they'll do, or if they'll do anything. I know I have to say them, though, and that it has to be now and it has to be here, while I'm still in The Before.

I open my car door and get out, quickly checking for traffic before running across the street. I feel my heart pounding as I get closer to the mailbox, open the lid, and drop the note inside. Then I run down the driveway and back across the street to my car before I can change my mind.

32

CHAPTER 32

I pull into my driveway about half an hour later. My heart isn't going crazy like it was when I left the note for Selena, but the late night and the early morning are catching up with me. I turn off the ignition, then lean back to rest my head against the seat and close my eyes. I'll just stay here for a couple of minutes, and then I'll go inside.

A light tap on my windshield makes me open one eye a few seconds later. I look at the glass in front of me, wondering what's fallen on it. I expect to see a leaf or maybe a twig, but that's not what's on my windshield at all. It's a white feather. It looks identical to the one that's on the floor of my car.

I still have no idea who the feathers are from, or what they mean. I stare at the feather on my windshield until I'm jarred out of my thoughts by the sound of my cell phone ringing. Maybe it's because I'm sleepy and still feel like I'm floating, or maybe it's because I assume it's Riley calling me, but I answer it without looking at the screen.

"Hey you," I greet him.

"Hello." My phone starts to slide past my fingers and I fumble to catch it before it falls to the floor. It's not Riley.

"Aunt Sarah," I pause. "Um, hi."

Hearing my aunt's voice is the last thing I expected. My mouth clamps shut, even though I have dozens of questions running through my mind.

"Is everything all right?" she asks, after what feels like more than a minute of silence on the line.

"Uh, yeah. I was just about to ask you the same thing." I have to wonder if I'm dreaming this. The way we left things when I kicked her out of my house, I was pretty sure I'd never be talking to her again.

"Your uncle is in surgery all day and asked me to check in with you, so..." her voice trails off.

"You can tell him that I'm fine."

More silence. I look out the car window, hoping either to be inspired for something that I can say, or for something I can use as an excuse to get off the phone.

"Look, the way we left things..." My aunt lets her voice trail off again, as though she expects me to say something. She's probably waiting for an apology.

"You mean the way you tried to boss me around in my own house and then force me to get on a plane with you?" I correct her. "The way you're trying to make me to go to college somewhere because it's some sort of family tradition, rather than what I want?"

She takes a breath, then exhales. "I think your uncle and I are both having trouble understanding what it is you want."

"To be in L.A. Is that so hard to understand?"

"For that boy who was at your house?"

"No," I tell her, but she clearly isn't listening because she interrupts me.

"We don't even know anything about him or what you're doing there, and you expect us to be okay with a sudden change in your college plans?"

I grit my teeth. "What I'm doing here is living my life. And as for that boy, his name is Riley. He's a journalism student at USC. He also writes novels and is working on one now. But that's not what you want to know, is it? You're probably more interested in what his parents do, where they live, and what their social status and income is. Am I right?"

"I actually just wanted to know if you're happy."

I freeze. She sounds serious. I know I should say something, but I can't.

"I know you think I'm an ogre, but I'm not." Her words are quiet and I hold my breath, straining to hear her.

"I don't—" I start my weak protest, but she keeps talking.

"I made a promise after your mother died that I would take care of you and keep you safe. I promised I'd protect you from harm in a way that I couldn't protect your mother. Seeing you take off for California and then change your mind about going to Harvard was like watching history repeat itself. I've been overbearing, but keeping you sheltered from a lot of the dangers in the world was the only way I knew how to keep my promise. I hope you know that."

"I'm sorry." It's probably the first time I've said those words to her.

There's a pause. She's probably as stunned to hear those words from me as I am to have said them.

"I see so much of your mother in you," she says after a moment.

Aunt Sarah rarely talks about my mother. The only times I've heard her mentioned was during conversations I was never sup-posed to hear about how she was the black sheep, and how if she'd never left Boston to move to California, then she'd never have met and married my father. That she'd still be alive if she'd been mature enough to not play the rebel. Of course my aunt couldn't know that my mother had to go, or that she was always supposed to meet up with my father. She doesn't know that their end together was their return to where they'd come from, or that where my mother went is where my aunt will also be one day. Only then will she understand what it all was for.

"I know you never approved of my mother leaving the world she was born into, just like you don't approve of me being here," I tell my aunt. I speak quickly so she can't interrupt me. "You don't run everyone's lives, though. You can't. Everyone has their own destiny."

There's silence on my aunt's end of the line. I expect a tirade to come next, or maybe even the click of the line going dead, since she's never been good with anything she sees as defiance.

"I know." The two softly spoken words nearly make me drop the phone again.

"You know?" I repeat.

"I do."

There's silence again, until my aunt speaks. "So back to your young man."

"Riley."

"Riley," she repeats. "Do you think he'd like to join us for dinner sometime, if your uncle and I come out for a visit?"

"A visit, or another kidnapping expedition?"

"A visit," she replies.

I'm quiet for a few seconds, trying to let her words sink in. My aunt sounds like she's actually giving in and accepting my decision. I was always certain that if something like this ever happened, it would surely be a sign of the coming apocalypse.

"I'll ask him," I finally say.

"It's just that—" She pauses and I can tell she's struggling with what to say. "I just always wanted to be a writer," she finishes. Her words tumble out and echo in my mind. This can't possibly be coming from the Aunt Sarah I know.

Maybe you don't know her like you think you do, I hear Noah say.

"I'd like to talk to him about his novels, if he doesn't mind," my aunt continues. "There are a few stories I put away in a drawer years ago, and I think I'd like to take them out again."

"You write?" I hope my words don't sound as shocked as I feel. Novel writing has never really seemed as high up there for my aunt as classical piano lessons and being the center of a ladies' social circle.

"There's a lot you don't know about me. That's probably my fault."

"I'd like to know more about your writing and whatever else you want to tell me about." My voice is barely audible, even to me.

Across the miles that separate us, I'm sure I feel her smile. It's the best conversation we've had since she and my uncle took me in after my parents were gone. I know she won't get the chance to tell me about her ambitions, her younger life, or her dreams and where they went until decades from now, when she leaves this phase of life for The Life-After. When she gets there, she'll tell me, and I'll be able to tell her what this life was really for.

It doesn't seem fair that all of this is going to end just as we're making this most tentative of connections. But there's nothing either of us can do to change it.

We hang up a couple of minutes later. My eyes go to the windshield in front of me and I look outside for a few minutes. I try not to think about how soon I'm going to be gone, or about all the things I won't get to say until those who are left here join me. It will be like the blink of an eye for me, but it will be years for them. I wish there was a way to make what's coming easier for my aunt and uncle, and for Riley. Most of all, I wish I could let them know that everything is going to happen exactly the way it's supposed to.

33

CHAPTER 33

Countdown to The Life-After: one week.

I think I'm in for a night of video games and Scrabble when Riley texts me to ask if he can come over. So when he parks his car in my driveway but leaves the engine idling, then gets out and walks up to my door, I'm a little confused.

"It's been a couple of years since driver's ed, but I'm pretty sure that even in California, you're supposed to turn the car off after—"

He presses a finger to my lips, cutting off the rest of my words. Then he lifts his finger away and leans in to kiss me. His arm circles my waist and he pulls me in close to him.

"Smart aleck," he tells me, when we break apart a minute later. "But an adorable one."

"You know, normally I don't like being interrupted mid-sentence, but—" And then his hands are cradling my face, his mouth covering mine again. He inches forward until we're as close as two people could be. My back presses against the wall and my arms wrap around him, somehow trying to squeeze him even more tightly against me even though there's no space between us. I have no idea how we're going to do anything tonight if this is what happens when I talk, but I'm not complaining. Not at all.

"You were saying?" He has the biggest, goofiest grin on his face, which just makes me want to kiss him again. I gulp for air, my breath coming in uneven bursts. I can't help but grin back once I start to breathe normally again. There are goose bumps all over my arms, and I swear even my hair has started tingling.

"Mmm, I was saying..." I blink hard, trying to clear my mind of the haze brought on by the feeling of his lips and his body pressed against me. From the look on his face, I can see I'm not alone. I have to move my eyes away from him to focus. When I see his car still idling in the driveway, I remember.

"Your car," I say. "It's still running."

"Then we'd better catch it," he teases, that heart-melting grin on his face again.

"Hmm?" I find myself swaying toward him but make myself stop. We're going to get a conversation in here, or at least I think we are. Unless I keep kissing him.

Conversation is overrated, my mind chimes in. I try to argue the point with myself, but come up with nothing. I think the tingling has short-circuited my brain.

"I want to take you somewhere." His hands move to my shoulders. One of his fingers traces circles on the bare skin of my neck. Tiny shivers run up and down my spine, and I can feel the little electric sparks of our energy where it meets.

"Somewhere?" I repeat.

Riley doesn't answer me while he lets his fingers move up to my jaw. We're not going anywhere if he keeps this up.

I try again. "Where?"

"It's a surprise." He raises an eyebrow, and I think he's trying to look mysterious. It makes me laugh. He kisses my forehead and then lets his hands drop to his sides. I don't really want them there, but it sure helps me think a little more clearly.

"Let me grab my keys before your car runs out of gas," I tell him.

Once I have my keys and my purse, he takes my hand and leads me outside. We stop beside the car for one more kiss before he'll open the passenger door for me. It's a good thing I don't have to stand for more than a few seconds after that.

"Why do I think you're taking me up to a city lookout to make out all night?" I ask him when he gets inside of the car.

"We're going somewhere way better than that." He turns the key in the ignition and then backs out of the driveway onto the road.

"Give me a hint?"

"Nope." He reaches over and touches my knee, then brings his hand back to the steering wheel.

I can tell from the streets he takes that we're headed away from Hollywood and out toward the San Fernando Valley. My suspicion is confirmed when we get onto the I-5 and head north of the city. I wrack my brain trying to figure out what's out this way.

"We're going to Six Flags?" I guess.

I hear a quiet laugh. "We're driving past Six Flags."

"You really aren't telling me where we're going?" I stick out my bottom lip, pretending to pout. This just makes him laugh harder when he glances over at me.

"Nope, so you might as well just enjoy the ride."

He takes a hand off of the steering wheel to reach over and press one of the stereo buttons. The music of Lazy Monday fills the car and I'm brought back to the first time I saw Riley, not knowing who he was. I remember what I thought of him them. If I hadn't been sent here to help him, I would never have gotten to know him. It makes me wonder how many other great people I haven't gotten to know in this life.

But I have reasons, I remind myself. No regrets.

I watch the scenery pass for a few minutes before it occurs to me that this drive feels familiar somehow, in a way I'm having trouble placing. I stop trying to puzzle it out as I hear Riley singing along to the song that's blasting through the speakers, and I feel warmth spread through me at the sound of his rich voice. I study him as closely as I can without him knowing it.

His energy is fascinating tonight. It's bright and strong, extending far out around him, and all of it is reflected in the smile that hasn't left his face since he got to my house. Given the stop-and-go traffic we're in, I think swearing at some of the other drivers would be completely acceptable. Riley doesn't even notice them, as far as I can tell.

"Are we going some place you go a lot?" I ask.

"Not telling." His smile becomes almost smug, in a playful sort of way.

"How long are we driving for?"

He shakes his head at me. "Are you going to start asking me if we're there yet?" he teases.

"Maybe."

He moves a hand off of the steering wheel to squeeze my fingers. "Patience."

It's a sign on the side of the road that brings the memories I've been searching for into my mind with a force that nearly pushes me forward in my seat. I know why this drive feels familiar to me now, but I doubt it's possible we're going to the same place it used to take me. This is the route I used to follow on my trips out of the city to watch the stars at night the last time I lived in L.A., when I was Anna. There's a back road I loved deep in the valley, where the lights of the city seemed far enough away to be another world. It felt like the galaxy of stars and planets I could see in the sky shone just for me.

Riley steers the car to an exit off the interstate I know well. Each turn we make is one I've made before, until we're on the road I used to park my car on when I'd come out here to watch the night sky.

It's not nightfall quite yet, but the sky is starting to get darker. We drive past the spot where I used to park. After a couple of miles, he slows the car down and turns into a driveway I don't know. There's a small house in front of us.

"My lady," he says, unbuckling his seat belt. "We have arrived."

34

— · —

CHAPTER 34

"**W**here are we?" I look out the passenger window. A white feather drifts by, carried by the evening breeze. I'm sure it's another message for me, if I could only figure out what it means.

"Welcome to my family's cottage," Riley says, pulling my attention away from the feather. I stop looking out the window, turning my head back to him. "There's a meteor shower tonight, and the night sky out here is incredible. It's so dark that you can see stard—"

"Stardust," I finish with him. He gives me a surprised smile. "I love stardust."

His smile grows wider. "Just let me grab a few things from the trunk so we can go star watch." He reaches for the door handle.

"I'll help." I unbuckle my seat belt and get out of the car.

He pops open the trunk and I see a few bags inside of it. I peek into one of them and see pillar candles and plastic champagne flutes. There are blankets in the bag beside it, and a lantern and a cooler in the corner of the trunk. Riley grabs the lantern.

"What's in there?" I reach for the cooler. He doesn't say a word as I slide it closer and open the lid. There's a bottle of sparkling grape juice inside, submerged among melting ice cubes. He reaches across my arm to pluck the bottle out from the cooler and puts it inside of a bag.

"You planned this?" I ask. Even in the growing darkness, I see color rising to his cheeks.

"Shhh," he says, but he looks proud of himself. I want to grab him by the ears and kiss him until I can't breathe. I might do it, too, when his hands aren't full. No one has ever planned a night like this for me. Not in this life, and not in my life as Anna.

He turns on the lantern and shines it ahead of us. "Can you hold this for a second?" he asks, holding the lantern out to me.

I take it from him, and he reaches inside of the trunk to lift out the two bags. With a bag on either arm, he closes the trunk again and reaches out a hand for the lantern.

"You have your hands a little full," I point out. "I've got this."

I aim the lantern's beam in front of us and let him the lead the way. He looks ahead to where it lights up our path, careful to guide us over the tree roots sticking out above the ground and holding back branches for me. He stops when we get to a clearing and sets the bags down.

"Can you shine that over here?" He points at a spot in front of him. I swing the lantern beam over to it.

He pulls a blanket out from one of the bags and spreads it over the ground, careful not to let it pick up any leaves or dirt. The champagne flutes are next, and then the bottle of sparkling grape juice. A second blanket appears from the same bag as the first. He leaves it folded up and puts it on top of the blanket that's already on the ground. The candles are put into glass jars and placed on the ground, close to the blanket. Removing a lighter from his pocket, he kneels down beside the candles to light each one. Then he stands up and walks back over to me, taking the lantern from my hands and setting it down beside the blanket.

He moves closer to me until our foreheads touch. His mouth grazes mine and I suck in my breath, holding it while his tongue runs across my lower lip. Then both of his lips are crushed against mine, my tongue finding his. I hold onto him, my hands grabbing onto his shirt at first and then somehow finding their way underneath it to press against his skin.

"This is dangerous," he murmurs, his lips still touching mine. "I shouldn't kiss you."

I know what he means. Being alone together in the middle of nowhere without any light but the lantern, the candles, and the stars makes this seem like a fairy tale. If he keeps kissing me like this, we might never stop.

"Then don't," I whisper. I feel him smile.

"Is that a challenge?" His moves his head so his mouth is just barely above mine.

"If it is, I'll bet you fail." My hands are still under his shirt, holding him close to me.

"Hmm." His lips move down to my jawline. I want to sink down onto the blankets, but his hands come to my elbows, steadying me. "Funny how failing feels like winning."

He raises his head, moving it a few inches away from mine. I can hear how quick his breathing is and realize my breath sounds the same. He closes his eyes.

"You can see the stars now," he says after a minute, opening his eyes again. He sits down on the blanket and pats the spot beside him. I sit, too.

He reaches for the bottle of juice and opens it. I hand him the champagne flutes and he pours each of us a glass, then hands one to me.

"To meteor showers and stardust," he says, raising his glass to mine.

"To the best night ever," I reply, clinking his glass. I mean it, too. This is the happiest I can ever remember feeling in my time here as Cassidy or as Anna. I take a sip of the juice, letting the bubbles slide down my throat. Riley reaches for my hand and we both lie back, looking up at the sky.

"I can never get over how beautiful it is," I murmur, looking up at the millions of tiny lights against the growing darkness.

"More than beautiful." Riley's voice is husky. I turn my head to him and see that he's not watching the sky. He's staring at me. His eyes lock with mine and there's a pull between us that grows until our bodies are curled together, my hips pressed against his.

It starts with a kiss on my earlobe and his thumb stroking my cheek. Then I'm below him, his lips tracing my collarbone and leaving a trail of kisses up my neck and chin. I don't realize I'm holding my breath until he pauses, hovering above me. I trace his mouth with my finger and he captures the tip of it between his lips, holding my eyes with his. I let my hand fall to the ground and his lips finally meet mine.

Maybe it's because I'm too caught up in a feeling that's more blissful than anything I've felt in The Before, or maybe part of me just intentionally forgets, but I don't connect with The Life-After when Riley takes me home late that night. When I remember the next morning, I still don't connect.

35

CHAPTER 35

Countdown to The Life-After: two days.

Time in The Before is a tricky thing. Sometimes it seems unending, like being in a constant state of waiting for something while the second hand on the clock just barely inches forward. Other times it seems to rush by, and it seems crazy that an entire day has already passed since waking up and that it's time to go to sleep again. Time is so carefully measured here in The Before, down to the nanosecond. It's like we're all grasping for control of something we can never hold onto.

I've spent most of my time here as Cassidy wishing for the years to fly by, so I can return to The Life-After. I've dreamed of the moment I'll be part of the lights and colors forever, never having to come back here. Now I'm almost there and I don't feel the way I always thought I would. There are less than forty-eight hours to go, and now I find myself wishing for more time.

I should be happy all of this is almost over. I know what I'm going back to and that the job I came here for is done. Riley's heart and energy are open and flowing, and his life will unfold the way it's supposed to. The Life-After won't need to cut this life short for him, and he won't need to come back here as a second-timer. Or that's what Noah keeps saying, anyway.

What I know, though, is after I leave, nothing between Riley and me will ever be the same. We'll meet again in the Life-After, but by then he'll have gone on to love someone else in a way that's deeper than what he feels for me right now. I think about waking up next to him this morning, and about his sleepy smile and the soapy scent of his skin. How I tingle when my energy connects with his. The light shining in his eyes over breakfast, and the feel of his lips on mine. The pure joy rushing through me that I can see in my energy.

"Noah?" I call out from where I sit on the sofa, expecting him to show up in my living room at any moment. I wait, but there's only silence.

"I need to talk to you." More silence, even though I know he must hear me.

I want to stay. I don't speak the words aloud, but it takes less than a second for Noah to appear in front of me.

"About time," I mutter.

"It was hard to hear you. Now I see why." He walks over to the armchair across from me and sits down.

I don't say anything, waiting instead for him to infuse me with his energy like he did the night that I blacked out. The infusion doesn't come. I have to look twice to make sure I'm seeing what I think I am. Instead of bringing his energy closer to me, Noah's pulling it farther away.

"What are you doing?" I ask. I try to connect my energy to his, but I'm not strong enough. I see the sparks get a little duller and move an inch closer around me.

There's no mistaking the disbelief on Noah's face, or the disappointment in his eyes. He doesn't even try to hide it. Great. A lecture from him is the last thing I need right now.

"I should ask you the same thing," he answers. "You haven't been connecting."

"No, I haven't been. I want to stay."

Telling him that is sure to make him boost me with some of his energy. When I don't feel anything, I look up at him. He's watching me.

"I can't stop you," he says.

He's my advisor, though. If anyone could stop me, it's him. In fact, I'm pretty sure he has to stop me. I'm telling him I want to break one of the rules.

"Wanting to stop you and being able to stop you are two different things," he continues, putting his hands into his suit coat pockets. "You have the free will to let your energy level drop to the point that even I can't reach you. I just hope you don't forget."

"Forget what?"

"What you went through before you left here the first time. Or do I need to remind you?"

I don't answer him. I can't even focus on forming words. My body clenches and I try to fight the feeling that's making my muscles seize everywhere, but it's stronger than I am. Then I realize where it's coming from.

"What are you doing?" I croak. There's pain shooting through me in so many places that I don't know where it starts or ends. Everything blurs around me and the pain keeps getting stronger. I'd crawl out of my own body if I could. Then I see myself as Anna, flashes of lights and sound everywhere around me. My breath comes in gasps until I choke and fall forward to the floor.

Stop. I can't open my mouth to speak, but Noah hears me. The feeling stops almost as quickly as it started. I keep my eyes closed while I wait for my pulse to slow down, my hands balled into fists. My fingernails dig into the flesh of my palms.

"Please don't ever do that again," I say, opening my eyes. I can barely hear my own voice.

"I hope I don't have to remind you again." If he feels even a tiny bit bad for what he just did to me, his face doesn't show it.

"You don't," I assure him. "I remember it well." The searing last days of being Anna before I blacked out on the road, caught in a memory, and went into the rocks. The last time I could breathe before it all went dark and I woke up to see the colors and the lights.

"I don't think you remember it well enough," he replies. "If you did, you wouldn't be doing what you're doing."

I'm silent for a minute. "I don't understand this," I finally say.

"Which part?"

The thought of leaving in two days aches in a way I can't quite put into words. Still, I have to try.

"You want me to love him. You want him to love me. You said that's why I'm here, so he can open his heart and connect with other people again. And he is."

Noah nods. "You've done your job well. You should be proud of yourself."

I ignore him, because pride is the last thing I feel right now. "So why are you asking me to break his heart?" And why are you asking me to break my heart all over again? I don't speak my last thought, but I know he hears me.

He presses the tips of his fingers together, looking at something in the space between them. The seconds tick past while the clock in the room keeps count. I wonder if he'll answer me.

It takes fifty-seven ticks of the second hand on the clock, but he does. "There's a difference between loving selfishly and loving truly, but you might not see it. I want to show you something."

36

CHAPTER 36

I steel myself for something like what he just put me through, but the sensation I dread doesn't arrive. Instead, everything gets blurry again. I squint, wondering what's wrong with my eyes until Noah and the room we're in fades away, and a clear picture forms in front of me.

Riley stands a few feet away, looking older than he does now—maybe ten years older. There's a gold band on the ring finger of his left hand, and his right hand holds the hand of someone else. When I look closer, I see it's me. I'm wearing a gold band on my left hand, too. A little girl bounces around on the living room floor in front of us. She has Riley's eyes and my dark hair, and I guess that she's our daughter. We look like a happy family.

The scene shifts out of focus and now I see something different. Riley looks a couple of years older than he did in the last vision, but it's hard to tell because his face is scrunched up, mangled in what looks like pain or maybe grief. Our daughter wanders around the living room, not seeming to notice anything around her. Tears stream down her face.

"She left us," Riley keeps saying. I see his mom sitting on a chair, watching him. Deep worry lines are etched across her face. She gets up from the chair and reaches her arms out for her granddaughter.

The image fades and now I'm watching someone's funeral. Is it mine? I try to get a closer look at the casket at the front of the room. The first thing I see is a man's suit jacket, then a sandy-blond head.

It's not me inside the casket. It's Riley.

Like scattered puzzle pieces coming together, it all starts to make sense. I stayed here in The Before, but met my end in a way similar to what I imagine happened to David. I simply disappeared without explanation, The Life-After catching up with me after I broke one of the rules to make sure I couldn't interfere in anyone else's fate. And what David's disappearance did to me when I was Anna, ending in my cosmic accident, is what my disappearance would do to Riley. I don't know what losing both of her parents would do to our daughter, and it's not something my heart can handle seeing right now. I open my eyes and look at Noah.

"What happens if I go?" I whisper.

"You already know," he answers. "It's the reason you're here."

"I want to see it." It's more than a want. It's as though I need to see Riley's future playing out in front of me so I can know he'll be happy and successful. I want to see that he'll do incredible, beautiful things. If I can see it and hold the vision with me, then maybe this won't be so hard.

"Close your eyes."

I do as I'm told. Within seconds, images that look like still photographs flash by, one after another. There's a book signing, first. Riley's at a table, surrounded by a mob of people. In the next image, he looks like he's receiving some type of award. After that there's a benefit concert where he's singing into a microphone, with John behind him on stage. It's followed by a series of dinners and fundraisers with politicians and celebrities. Then he's on another stage at a podium, speaking at an event with thousands of people. The banners tell me it's for a humanitarian charity.

The images fade out and I see him inside of a beautiful house. From the view that's outside of the floor-to-ceiling windows, I can tell he's high up in the Hollywood Hills. He looks content, his arm around another little girl who appears to be about three or four years old.

She doesn't look like the girl in my vision of the two of us, but I can tell this is his daughter. He's reading to her, and there's delight all over her face. Pure joy and love are written across his.

He looks up from the book for a moment, his eyes moving to the doorway of the room. What he sees there makes his eyes light up even more. I try to follow his gaze and think I see a woman standing in the doorway who must be his wife, but the scene fades away before I can make out what she looks like. Then Noah is standing in front of me again.

"He stays happy?" I ask. "He has a good life?" I already know the answer to both questions.

Noah nods. "He has the life he's supposed to. It's all because you opened his heart to love again."

"What happens after I'm gone, though? He doesn't close off again?" I know the answer to this, too, but for some reason I need to ask.

"No. He's filled with grief at first, of course, because he doesn't know what's next for you. From that grief, though, will come something he writes in your memory. The book will lead him to meet his wife and will also start his rise to fame. It will only take a few months from the time you return to The Life-After for him to cross paths with the woman he'll marry. His energy will connect with hers, and that connection will stay and strengthen. He'll know he has to see her again, and that she's the one for him."

It's hard not to flinch at the thought of Riley marrying someone else. I try to hide it, but it doesn't work. Noah takes another step closer to me, his voice softer than I've ever heard it.

"I can't stop you from making your own choice, but I'm asking you to let yourself be guided by love. Don't make a choice based on selfishness or fear."

"Are you going to boost me?" I ask, staring at the floor. I can't look at him.

"Not tonight."

I raise my head, not sure I'm hearing him correctly. I can feel how low my energy is now, and I'm sure Noah can sense it, too. I have to be close to blacking out.

"I can't force you back to The Life-After, so there's no point in me boosting you now. If you choose not to connect tonight, your energy will probably get so low that you won't be able to connect again even if you want to. This is your decision to make."

I sink down onto the sofa, watching him disappear from the room. I know he isn't kidding. It's especially important for me to raise my energy now, so I can be ready for what's supposed to happen in two days. I also have the choice to sever that connection and stay until The Life-After catches up with me and banishes me from existence. Just like David.

Staying means having a chance I didn't have in my time here as Anna, though. I'll have the time to explore a love unlike anything I've ever had, even if it's only for a little while. If I stay, I'll feel Riley's arms around me again and see his smile. The kisses we'll share when I see him tomorrow won't be our last. Thinking about leaving knocks the air right out of my lungs.

But I know what's waiting for me in The Life-After. I know what I'd tell everyone here in The Before, if I could. The Life-After is the next phase, and it's filled with a love that's even brighter than anyone could imagine. Leaving The Before isn't an ending at all, but a beginning. There's no reason to be sad, or to mourn or grieve. There's no loss, only gain and a lot to celebrate. I recite this to myself, but it doesn't make it easier.

I know that if I stay, I'll ruin Riley's chance at an easy transition to The Life-After. When I disappear like David did—and everything Noah has shown me lets me know I will—Riley's time here in The Before will be beyond repair. He'll be devastated, beyond the help of anyone, and he'll have to die. Our daughter will know the kind of pain that no little girl should ever have to know. Two lives will be left in shambles, and Riley will be forced to come back as a second-timer, all because I made a choice to stay and experience this kind of romantic love for a few more years.

I know what interfering with fate can do. I can't do that to Riley, no matter what the thought of returning to The Life-After is doing to me right now. Love means not ripping away the life and happiness someone else is destined for, even if it feels like it's tearing my own heart into a million pieces.

I lean back against the sofa cushions, listening to the ticking of the clock. Then I close my eyes and connect to The Life-After.

CHAPTER 37

Countdown to The Life-After: one day.

I look at my hands and my arms, uncertain about what I expect to see. My skin is still the same pale shade it's always been. I wiggle my fingers and then run them through my hair before dropping my arms at my sides. I'm here and I'm whole. No one would ever know by looking at me that I'm going to die in less than twenty-four hours. I keep scanning my body up and down, though, searching for some clue that could give everything away.

The only difference I've seen so far is in my energy. The spot that's been dead for so long has had tiny threads of color running through it today, and I presume it's something The Life-After is doing to help me get ready to go back. I haven't asked Noah about it, because I'm not sure it matters. That, and I've been too busy thinking about the evening ahead of me to give it much thought.

Tonight is the last time I'll see Riley here in The Before. I smooth a wrinkle in my dress and glance at myself in the mirror. The girl staring back looks nervous, and she jumps when the doorbell rings. I see myself shiver. There's a full-blown swarm of butterflies in my stomach by the time I pull open the front door.

"Hi." My voice cracks on the single syllable. I hide my hands behind my back to conceal my trembling fingers, and take a step to the side so Riley can come in.

When he walks through the door, I notice the rose in his hand. He holds it out to me. I try to keep my hand steady when I take it from him.

"Thank you," I say, barely able to put the two words together. When he leans in to kiss me and pulls me closer to him, I'm sure it has to be obvious that I'm shaking. Maybe he doesn't notice, though, because he moves a hand up to my hair and twirls a strand of it around his finger. When I look at him, his eyes shining down at me, I know this is going to be the hardest couple of hours I've ever lived through.

He reaches down for the hand that's not holding the rose. His touch gives me enough strength to make the trembling stop. With our fingers entwined, I lead him into the kitchen where I've already started dinner.

"It smells good in here," he says, sniffing the air. "Spaghetti?"

"Close," I tell him. "Spaghetti squash." He looks confused so I point at the yellow spaghetti squash that's in a baking dish on the counter.

"We're putting tomato sauce on that?" he asks. I can tell he's not big on the idea.

"Have you ever had a spaghetti squash?" I ask.

"It's a vegetable, right?"

"You do shop and cook for yourself, right?" I tease him, holding up the squash.

"Of course I do. I'm the king of mac and cheese and frozen pizza."

I swat him. "Liar, you helped me chop up vegetables when we had lunch here."

"That's salad. Anyone can make a salad."

"What have you lived on since moving out?" I challenge.

"Takeout and family dinners?" he asks, giving me his best lost-little-boy expression.

I look up at the ceiling. "Hopeless."

He laughs, putting his arms around me. "Thank you for making dinner," he says, burying his head in my hair. The number of butterflies in my stomach multiples by at least two hundred, and tears well up in my eyes. I swallow hard and concentrate on silently counting to ten, trying to get it together.

Once dinner is ready, we bring our plates to the living room and eat in front of the TV. When our plates are empty and our stomachs are full, we settle in against the sofa cushions, changing channels until we get to one that's showing a movie. It takes me a minute before I realize we're watching Ghost.

The movie was released before I existed asCassidy, but when I was Anna, I had friends who worked as extras on-set during the filming. I was in The Life-After by the time it hit the theaters, but I've seen it and I know what it's about. I don't know if Riley does, and I can't see him being all that crazy over watching a movie about love that carries on after death.

"Have you seen this?" I ask him.

"Yeah." There's a far-off look in his eyes, and I wonder if this movie reminds him of Amanda. I do a quick check of his energy. It isn't retreating away from me or closing in around him. If anything, his energy is getting stronger as it stays connected with mine.

"Let's watch something a little happier tonight," I suggest, easing the remote control from his hand. I stop changing channels when I land on the first safe movie I see.

"Palm Springs?" he asks, his lips curving into a smile.

"Humor me." I lean forward to put the remote on the table and then I snuggle into him, letting my head rest against his chest. He puts his arms around me, rubbing his thumb against the top of my hand.

I pretend to watch the movie until I feel Riley shift beside me, gently tugging on my hand as he lies down on his side. I think he means for me to lie against him, both of us facing the TV, but I turn around to face him instead. He looks at me and I bring both of my hands up to cradle his face. I move as close as I can to him and cover his mouth with mine.

I don't know how many minutes pass while I kiss him. My hands move down to grip his shirt and I'm choking back tears again, along with a lump in my throat, when I realize this is the last time I'll ever get to kiss him like this. I'm not sure how I'm going to let him go and so I kiss him harder, pulling the fabric of his shirt up and then bringing my lips to his stomach, touching them to his skin. Then his shirt is just gone and I'm leaving a trail of kisses from his navel to his neck, my mouth moving up to tug on his earlobe. He sucks in his breath and before I know it, I'm under him and he's on top of me, his tongue dipping into my mouth as his body presses against mine. I try to bring my arms around him but find them pinned down by my dress straps, which have dropped from my shoulders to my upper arms.

"Arms," I say, when we come up for air.

He sits up, alarmed. "Did I put too much weight on you?" he asks.

"No, it's my dress." I reach for one of my wayward straps. "I couldn't move my arms."

He catches my fingers and moves them away from the strap. Then he reaches behind me and I feel the zipper of my dress slide open. He pauses.

"Is this okay?" he asks.

My heart pounds in my ears. "Yes," I whisper, slipping my arms out of the loosened dress and letting it fall to my waist. I could let it stay there, I know, but I don't. My dress ends up on the floor beside his shirt.

It shouldn't be any different than when we've hung out in my pool, I tell my racing mind. My bra and underwear cover just as much as my bikini did then. And it's not like we haven't been making out for the last two weeks. But when his hands caress my shoulders and he brings his lips to my jaw, I know that if I let it, this could go way past where we've been.

His finger traces a line from my belly button up to my chest and back down again, coming to rest against the inside of my thigh. A shiver runs through me, and it's the anticipation of what could come next that forces me to break away from him.

His eyes open. I sense there's an unspoken question tugging at the corner of his lips, and it causes me to shift my gaze away from him. It would be so easy to keep going, especially since we'll never have this chance again. I take a deep and unsteady breath, which helps my mind clear for just long enough to hear the nagging voice inside my head remind me that the heavier this gets, the more gut-wrenching tomorrow is going to be for both of us.

"We don't have to rush into anything, you know," he says, and I know he's misread my shiver and why I'm not looking at him now. He drops a kiss on the top of my head. "We have lots of time."

Except we don't. Being reminded of this is pretty much the same as being doused with ice water.

"We do," I lie. It's a struggle to keep my voice from quivering. I'm not sure if I'll regret this choice for all eternity, or if I will be proud of myself for choosing to not make things that much worse.

I force myself to sit up and watch Riley lean over to grab his shirt from the floor. I reach for my dress, trying to hide my face from him because if he sees it, he'll know I'm barely keeping it together.

"You look so serious," he says, as I get dressed. "That definitely wasn't my plan."

I force a smile to my lips, reminding myself that I can't let my mind skip ahead to tomorrow while he's here. If I think too much about these being my last few hours with him, then I might break. I can't do that in front of him.

"Not serious," I tell him. "I'm just a little more tired than I thought. My yoga class today was pretty intense." I reach for his hand and squeeze it.

"Back to the movie, then?" he asks.

"There was a movie?" I feign innocence. Watching a movie kind of sounds like torture to me right now, when I know we could still be doing what we were doing. He laughs and picks up the TV remote, rubbing my back with his free hand.

I try to act as though I'm paying attention to what's on the screen, but I have no idea what I've been watching when the credits finally roll. The clock on the wall tells me it's only just after 10 p.m. It's early, but I'm still a lot less steady than I should be tonight. I need to keep control of my energy, and I know I won't be able to do that if Riley remains here for much longer. If I don't control it, I'm not sure I'll be able to go through with what I need to do in the morning. So I do the only thing I can think of and make a production out of faking a yawn. It doesn't go unnoticed.

"Sleepy girl?" Riley asks. He sits up beside me and brings his fingers to my chin, tilting it upward.

"Mmm-hmm," I answer, closing my eyes.

He drops a kiss on the top of my head. "I'm sleepy, too," he admits. "I was in the studio at five this morning."

I can tell he wants me to ask him to stay here tonight. The only thing in the world that I want right now is more time with him and to feel him sleeping next to me, but I know it can't happen. I'll want to keep doing what we were doing before, and I won't be able to keep my energy steady. I also won't be able to explain why I'm getting up before the sun rises to drive to Malibu.

"I think I'm going to go to sleep early tonight," I tell him.

"That's probably not a bad idea for me, either." He kisses the top of my head again. I want to grab him by the ears and make out with him until the sun comes up, but I kiss the tip of his nose instead. Then I stand up and reach for one of the plates we left on the table. He stands up, too, helping me clear the dinner dishes from the living room.

When I pretend to be so tired that I can barely keep my eyes open, he takes that as his cue to head home. I walk with him to the front door, trying not to think about this being the last time we'll say goodnight.

I linger behind him in the foyer, silent while he puts on his shoes and reaches for the door handle. He pauses after cracking the door open, and then turns to face me again. He sweeps me up in the gentlest, sweetest goodnight kiss I've ever had, and it takes almost everything I have not to break down into sobs and beg him to stay.

"I'll call you tomorrow," he promises before he walks out the door.

I close the door behind him and then sink down to the floor. The tears I've been fighting back all night spill down my cheeks, and I don't try to stop them this time.

38

CHAPTER 38

Countdown to The Life-After: day zero.

In the entire time I've been back here in The Before, I've never hoped morning wouldn't come. But at 2 a.m., after I've been lying awake in my bed for hours, I wish time would stand still. I breathe in slowly, trying to clear the image of Riley out of my mind. I can't think about him now. If I do, every part of me will want to go back on the decision I've made. My love has to be stronger than my fear of what's going to change.

All I can do in these last hours is try to stay calm. I pull myself up to sit cross-legged, my back propped up against the pillows on my bed, and put the tips of my index fingers and thumbs together. Resting my hands on my knees, I focus on my breath as Amarleen taught me to do.

It feels as though my eyes have been closed for only a few seconds when I bolt awake, my head jerking up from where it's fallen forward. Every one of my limbs tingles, and the energy is so strong that my spine feels like a live wire. It takes me a minute or two to catch my breath and settle into the energy.

When I look over at the clock, I see that three hours have passed since I last checked the time. There's also something on my bedside table that wasn't there before—an indigo feather.

Thanks, Noah, I think. He's here with me, I know, even though I can't see him. I will soon.

I rub my eyes with my hands, fighting back a yawn. It's time to get out of bed for the last time in The Before, but it takes a lot of effort. My body doesn't want to cooperate with me, or maybe it's me who doesn't want to cooperate with myself.

"A little help, please," I whisper into the still-dark room. Then I'm standing, effortlessly, putting a comb through my hair and getting dressed. My clothes are the ones I'll be found in when my body is pulled out of the ocean.

The streets are empty when I leave my house to drive to Malibu, since it's still too early for most people to be up. It will look like I went for an early morning run on the beach, and then maybe waded into the waves to cool off. Even at sunrise, it's already a blisteringly hot day. Everyone will think it was all just a tragic accident that happened to a young girl who didn't know about the riptide.

I park my car in a deserted beachside parking lot. Once I'm on the beach, I jog for about a mile, leaving footprints in the sand. I'm doing my best not to think about Riley when I pass by the spot where he left the bouquet of pink roses that morning a couple of weeks ago. The flowers aren't there anymore but I'm reminded that Amanda must have walked this way too, maybe also trying to keep Riley from her mind.

I stop jogging as the first rays of daylight hit the beach and I get to the spot where I need to be. Dropping to my knees in the sand, I let the sound of the ocean waves fill my ears. I close my eyes. Soon the golden glow of The Life-After is all I can see, the light stronger than it's ever been since I left to come back as a second-timer.

The glow remains around everything when I open my eyes again. Noah is here now. I glimpse him standing by the shore.

"Ready?" he asks, reaching for my hand.

"Ready," I echo, letting my fingers join his.

I put one foot in front of the other, keeping hold of Noah's hand while we head for the ocean. My feet meet the water and I feel as if I'm floating on top of it, even though I wade deeper into it with each step. I can't feel the temperature of the water, and I know I won't be aware of anything when I go under. When I'm waist deep, I look back to the shore for one final, silent goodbye.

Then I'm moving again, deeper and deeper until the water is at my shoulders. I start to bend my knees. The water is up to my eyebrows and I'm close to breathing it in when I feel myself being lifted up and carried somewhere high above the surface. It's only a few seconds until there's sand beneath my feet. When I open my eyes, I'm back on the beach. Noah is nowhere to be seen.

The shoreline and the cliffs around me are still outlined in golden light, so I know I haven't lost my connection to the energy of The Life-After. I look around for Noah again but still can't find him. What I do see makes me squint into the sunlight and wonder if I'm still submerged beneath the ocean's waves, having some kind of between-life dream. I can't possibly be seeing what I think I am, because what I see is David at the end of the beach. The breeze ruffles his dark, shaggy hair.

He walks closer to me and there's a smile playing on his lips. I should smile back, but my mouth, much like the rest of me, doesn't want to move. If I can reach out and touch him, then perhaps that will prove this is real. Still, my arms stay glued to my sides.

In the decades since I left my life here as Anna, and for most of the years since my return to The Before, I've imagined finding David. I've dreamed of disproving everything Noah told me about what happened to him once he vanished. I've wanted to believe that David's energy was here somewhere, lingering, because energy can't be destroyed. Every time I let myself have that daydream, though, I was so swept up in the relief and excitement of seeing him again that the feeling lasted even after the daydream was over. Now that the daydream is real—or I think it is, at least—relieved and excited isn't how I feel.

I know I loved David once, very much, and I'm sure a part of me still loves him. But it's different now. When I look at him standing in front of me, I don't feel the way I did back then and I can't come up with the words to tell him this. I don't need to, though, because he seems to hear my thoughts.

"It's okay," he says. "This is how it's supposed to be."

It seems like it's been forever since I last heard his voice. I want to know where he's been since he disappeared a lifetime ago, but something isn't letting me ask him.

"How did you get here?" I ask instead.

"You freed me." That's all he says.

"I don't understand."

He nods and reaches out to touch my arm. I expect to feel a tingle of energy like I do when Riley touches me and our energy connects, but I don't. When I focus, I discover it's because my energy isn't reaching out to connect with his. It should be. Our energy used to be linked so strongly that it destroyed me when I didn't have that connection to him anymore. Or at least that's how Noah explained it to me.

"This is how it's supposed to be," David repeats, answering my thoughts again. If he can hear them, then his energy must already be elevated to a level that's far above mine. This doesn't even begin to make sense.

He moves his hand away from my arm. I watch him, hoping something in his energy will tell me everything I want to know. It doesn't. Either I'm thinking that or it's clear what I'm trying to do, because he opens his mouth to speak again.

"When your energy began connecting with Riley's, my energy started to become free from where it was bound. The more you connected, little by little, the freer my energy became. When you opened yourself up fully and let yourself love again, what I did wrong was set right. Pardoned or forgiven, I guess, since your energy healed things. It's like I served my time and now I'm free to move on."

"You couldn't somehow tell me this as your energy was set free?" Maybe that's not how this works, but it seems like he would have been able to reach out to me.

He holds out one of his arms. "Do you recognize this?" he asks, opening his fist. A white feather lies flat on his palm. I stare at it.

"The feathers were from you?" I ask.

"Yes. They were all I could send when you started connecting with Riley."

A hand touches my shoulder, and I force my eyes away from David and the feather. Noah stands beside me.

"Are you ready?" he asks. I start to answer him, but then I realize he isn't speaking to me.

"I'm ready," David says.

I open my mouth to ask him what he's ready for, but he fades away in front of me and the feather flutters into the air. Within seconds, there's no sign he ever stood here on the beach, except for one white feather that's landed on the sand.

CHAPTER 39

"**W**hat just happened?" I keep my eyes on the spot where David disappeared.

Noah squeezes my shoulder. "He went home."

I shake my head, still not understanding.

"The Life-After," he explains.

"But I thought—" I stop. None of this feels real. "I don't get it," I mumble, letting myself sink down to sit on the sand. Noah sits down beside me.

I watch the ocean, silent while I try to figure out how to say what I'm thinking. It's hard to find words that won't make me sound like a spiteful person who's finding the universe more than a little bit out of balance. Finally, I just say it.

"David gets to return to The Life-After because of something I did to set him free, and I have to abandon the kind of love that almost everyone else in The Before gets years to explore and enjoy? That's how this works?" I know I won't feel this way when I'm in The Life-After, but here in The Before, on this beach, it just seems messed up.

"Not quite," he replies.

"Then what?" I ask.

"It's not your time."

"But today is the day I go back," I argue. I'm certain it is. I've been counting down to this day for eighteen years.

"You thought so, but it's not," Noah says. He scoops up a handful of sand, letting it slip through his fingers. I watch it scatter in the breeze. "Today is the day you freed David."

"So when do I go back?"

"After you finish your life here with Riley."

"I can't see Riley past today, though. You already showed me what happens if I stay."

He scoops up another handful of sand. "No. You saw what you needed to see so you could make the decision on your own. You chose to be guided by a love for Riley that went beyond your own wants, so he could have the life he's meant for. That kind of choice is the truest love there is."

"I still want that for him, more than anything. I want him to get to The Life-After when he's supposed to, and to be happy for the rest of his time here."

"He'll do both of those things, but you're going to do them together."

I gape at Noah, not sure if I'm really hearing what I think I'm hearing. He smiles.

"Let me show you. Close your eyes and think of Riley. You'll understand."

He reaches out and takes my hand. I close my eyes. Golden light glitters for a moment and then images begin to appear. The first image is similar to something Noah has shown me before. Riley sits on a sofa, reading to a little girl who's about three or four years old. But this time, she's the daughter Riley and I had when I saw his future if I chose to stay, and not the girl I watched him read to in the other vision.

He looks up from the book, just like he did the last time I saw this. When his eyes move to the doorway of the room, I can now see the woman standing there. It's me, and I'm holding a baby boy who appears to be only a few months old. There's a gold band on the ring finger of my left hand, I notice. Riley has one, too.

His eyes light up when he sees me standing there with our son. I walk over to sit beside him and our daughter, holding our son on my lap, and we read the story together. Our daughter's eyes shine with delight when Riley makes up voices for each of the characters. On my face, I see deep contentment and love.

The image fades and what I recognize as a film set comes into focus. There's a whole crew of people on the soundstage, and I can tell from how much time I spent on sets as Anna that everyone is getting ready to shoot a scene. I can't figure out why I'm being shown this image until I notice a young woman sitting in the corner, waiting as a makeup artist finishes touch-ups to her face. The young woman is me.

I go back into acting? I wonder, just as the scene fades out and another image takes its place. Riley is with me this time, and we make our way from a limousine onto a red carpet. Flashbulbs light up the night and I blink a few times, but I'm grinning from ear to ear and so is Riley. We wave at the people standing behind metal barricades on either side of the red carpet. Then we continue over to a step-and-repeat backdrop for photos and interviews where we're greeted by a slew of photographers, videographers, and reporters. One of the reporters holds his microphone out to me and the scene fades.

It's replaced by the image I've seen before of Riley at a book signing, with hundreds of people crowding around him. The line of people waiting to talk to him and get his signature wraps around the store several times. I feel a surge of pride watching him scribble inside of the novel that's handed to him. He beams as he passes it back across the table. Selena is there, too, standing beside me. We must make up and become friends again. Maybe the note I left in her mailbox was the start.

Right after that comes the image of Riley receiving an award, and then the benefit concert where he's on stage singing, and he receives wild cheers from the thousands of people in the audience. I see flashes of fundraising dinners and charity events similar to the ones I saw before, but both of us are there this time.

When the familiar pictures fade, a new one flashes before my eyes. We're older now, probably in our fifties. Our daughter and son sit with us at a dining room table, along with a baby in a high chair. A young man I haven't seen before sits beside our daughter, and both of them wear wedding bands. This is our son-in-law and the baby is our grandson. It's a vision of a life I didn't think was possible, and that I can't wait to live.

Golden light appears in front of me again, and its brilliant glow is all I can see. I open my eyes, and then I blink a few times to bring myself back to the present. Noah studies me.

"This is different from what you showed me before," I tell him. Of course he already knows that.

"It is," he agrees. "Like I said, what you saw before was what you needed to see to listen to your heart, instead of being overpowered by the fear of what you stood to lose. It's all energy."

I think about that for a minute, and then about all I've just seen. A life with Riley, and our children and grandchildren. A friendship with Selena again. Doing great things for the world to raise the energy of others and of ourselves. Having the successful career that was cut short when my time in The Before as Anna came to an end. Another chance at this part of life and at love, blessed with all of the things I never thought I would have.

"Take a few minutes to process it," Noah says, squeezing my shoulder again. I turn to face him and for the first time that I can remember, wrap my arms around him in a hug.

"Thank you," I murmur, my voice coming out muffled since my face is pressed into his shoulder. He puts his arms around me.

"Welcome back to life."

40

— • —

CHAPTER 40

It's still early in the morning when I rap my knuckles against Riley's door. I know I'm probably waking him up, but something inside of me wants to see him right now and can't wait a couple more hours. I know I have the rest of my life here and in The Life-After to spend with him, but part of me needs to be sure everything that's happened today isn't just my mind playing some huge prank. If I can see Riley and hold him, then I'll know this is real.

I've barely touched the door when it opens. He's disheveled from sleep and bleary-eyed, but Riley's face still lights up when he sees me. His smile sends warmth through me from head to toe. I take a step forward into his arms. He smells good, like sleep and fabric softener and a hint of soap. The scents mingle together and comfort me in a way I know nothing else can.

"Did I wake you up?" I ask him, burying my head in his shoulder.

His arms tighten around me. I feel him shake his head. "Something woke me up a while ago, and I couldn't get back to sleep." He takes my hand and leads me inside. I push the door closed behind us.

We stop by the kitchen, where Riley presses his lips against my forehead. "Coffee?" he asks.

I bring a finger up to his bottom lip, touching it gently. He kisses my finger, and then wraps his arms around my waist.

"Let's go back to sleep," I suggest.

He nods, taking my hand again and leading me past the kitchen and into his bedroom. I sink down onto his bed, burrowing under the covers and holding them up for him to slide in next to me. Lying beside him was all I wanted to do last night when I thought I was leaving. Now I know I'll be doing this for the rest of our lives.

He doesn't ask me why I've shown up at his door not long after dawn. And then I realize something. I'm not sure if I get it on my own, or if it's Noah who puts the thought into my head, but it doesn't matter. Riley wants me to be here, and he doesn't care what time it is or why I came. And here is where I always want to be, snuggled up like we are right now, so close I can feel the rise and fall of his chest. I relax against him.

"Comfortable?" he asks.

"Very," I say, yawning.

He kisses the top of my head and then lets his chin come to rest there. After a minute or two his breathing becomes deep and even, and I know he's fallen asleep.

When he wakes up, I'll tell him about the yoga weekend Lauren mentioned. I'll ask him if he wants to come with me, and if he wants to come to Amarleen's class some time. The thought of introducing the boyfriend I never thought I'd have to the new friends I also never thought I'd have makes me want to laugh. Not because it's funny, but because the surprises I've been given make me happy in a way I never could have imagined before. I have years of this happiness ahead of me now, and I'm grateful.

I shift my eyes to the window, just in time to see an indigo feather float by. It stays suspended in the air for a few seconds, held up against the glass.

Thank you, Noah, I think.

Now that I've finished my job as a second-timer, I don't know if I'll be able to see or hear Noah until we meet again in The Life-After. He'll always be here, though, watching over me.

A sunbeam streams in through the window, falling over Riley and me. The beautiful light of this new day is the last thing I see before my eyes close and I fall asleep in the place where I know I'm meant to be.

41

EPILOGUE

I have no game.

Cassidy probably thinks our fingers brushed together by accident, especially since I just chickened out and shoved my hands into my pockets. Smooth, right? I mean, I was only going to hold her hand. I wasn't asking her to marry me or something. It should have been natural at this point in the night, but I froze.

It wouldn't even be the first time I held her hand. We were palm to palm with our fingers laced together the night she was being harassed by a group of guys who anyone could see were bad news. It wasn't a romantic gesture that evening, but me playing the part of her boyfriend for a few minutes to make those sketchballs back off.

There was something I felt then that I still can't explain. It was as though tiny little sparks covered my fingers and palm for a second or two—and yeah, I know that sounds like it came straight from the script of a bad romantic comedy. Maybe those rom-coms are on to something, though, because it was enough to knock me off course. I've been thinking about that feeling, and about her, ever since.

I watch Cassidy now as she fumbles through her purse, looking for something. Is she embarrassed? Relieved? Did she even notice I reached for her hand? A strand of her chestnut hair falls in front of her face before I can read her expression.

"Lose something?" I ask, mostly to break the silence.

"Nope. I just want gum."

Cassidy doesn't look at me. She definitely noticed.

I don't remember if I ever had game, but it never used to matter. The one real relationship I've had in my nineteen years of life was with a girl I grew up with. There was no awkward getting-to-know-you phase with Amanda when we started dating, because we'd known each other since kindergarten. Reaching for her hand never made me nervous, and we got our first kiss out of the way in eighth grade during a game of spin the bottle. We just were, and I always knew where I stood.

Asking out someone I don't have years of history with is new to me, and I didn't even do that right the first time with Cassidy. Riley Davis. Call for emergencies. That's what I typed into her phone. Like the genius I am, I didn't ask her to text me her number. I also didn't ask her to get together or to take her out and show her around L.A., even though I wanted to.

Nope, I choked. My mind got caught up in all the reasons why anyone going on a date with me would be a horrible idea right now, and I watched her get into her car and drive away. Even with all of that, she was on my mind for hours that night and I wondered if she would text me. She didn't, but I got a second chance when we ran into one another at Amoeba Music soon after.

I didn't choke that time, but I also didn't ace it. I technically didn't say this was a date. I used her eighteenth birthday as my way around that, insisting she let me take her out to celebrate since she didn't have plans or any family in L.A. That's how we ended up at La Piazza tonight, dining on Italian food at an outdoor table overlooking a fountain and cobblestoned courtyard. Things were going well once both of us finally relaxed, until just now when I unlocked the Mighty Overthinker achievement badge over holding her hand of all things. I'm a mess.

"Riley?"

Cassidy's voice brings me back to the moment. I see hesitation in her sea-blue eyes.

"They're closing down here," I tell her, even though she already knows that. We were headed to my car when I made things weird. "We should go."

We still have to get through the drive back to her house. I wrack my brain for something brilliant to say that will lighten the mood, but nothing comes to mind.

Neither of us speaks until we're inside my car and I've started the engine. Someone up there must like me, because the song on the radio saves me from stumbling over my words and saying something ridiculous.

"Folk?" Cassidy asks as I back the out of the parking spot. "Let's try a rock station, maybe?"

I smirk, even though I want to bow down to whatever higher power has brought us back to more normal conversation. "It's on a rock station."

"What, did the music director blow out his eardrums at too many real rock shows?"

"Banjos are the new guitar solo," I tease her. "What cave have you been living in?"

"One with much better stations than this." She nearly jumps out of her seat in her hurry to change the station.

"Keep going," I warn her. "There's no EDM allowed in this car."

"Yet you allow indie folk and call it rock. This is a sad day for our friendship."

I could overthink her use of the word "friendship" while we're on a date, but I won't. Not right now, anyway, since I don't know if I should feel deflated over that or be grateful she's rescuing me from myself.

"Guess I won't be giving you my extra ticket to Bon Iver," I joke, naming the first indie folk artist that comes to my mind.

Cassidy scrunches up her nose. "I have to wash my hair that night, anyway."

"You don't even know what night it is," I point out.

"It doesn't matter."

This is more like it. I settle back against the driver's seat and guide the car up the winding roads through the Hollywood Hills that lead us to Cassidy's house. She and I exchange barbs the entire time, until I turn into her driveway.

I park the car and get out to open Cassidy's door. Our banter turns to silence while she gets out of the vehicle and leads me up the driveway. The evening breeze rustles through the trees just as some force outside of myself moves my hand to the small of her back. And there it is again—that feeling. I don't know what it is between us when I touch her, but every nerve ending in my body comes alive. I wonder if she feels it, too.

We're close to her front door when her shoe heel hits a dip in the driveway. I see her wobble and use my hand to steady her. She moves closer to me then, and her eyes lock with mine.

My fingertips come up to her chin before I realize what I'm doing. I hear a hitch in her breath as my head bends down, our lips drawing closer. We both know what comes next, or at least what should.

I haven't kissed anyone since my last kiss with Amanda, the night before she died. I haven't wanted or dared to until now. My heart hammers in my chest, and I feel the adrenaline kick in.

Don't mess this up, I tell myself. Still, it's all I can do to breathe.

Milton Keynes UK
Ingram Content Group UK Ltd.
UKHW032314121024
449481UK00011B/391